Act 1:
Chardonnay
&
Traces of Lipstick

Written By: Shawn Cupp

Acknowledgments

My mom, for always telling me to write a book instead of rap (RIP)

Hugh "Hank" Wilson, JR, see you when I get there (RIP)

Empire World Publishing, and a list of everybody with their author names instead of fb or nicknames.

If a girl walks in and carves her name in my heart"

"I'll turn and run away"

-Real Talk-Send Me An Angel

"I saw you this morning, you were moving so fast"

"Can't seem to loosen my grip, on the past"

"And I miss you so much, there's no one in sight"

-Leonard Cohen-In My Secret Life

May everyone live and may everyone die"

"Hello my love and my love, goodbye"

-Leonard Cohen-Here It Is

If it be your will, that I speak no more"

"And my voice be still, as it was before"

"I will speak no more"

-Leonard Cohen-If It Be Your Will

I'm turning tricks, I'm getting fixed"

"I'm back on Boogie Street"

-Leonard Cohen-A Thousand Kisses Deep

A Game Of Chance

The fact that I am here, alone with her, in and of itself is a miracle. She is the type of woman men like myself fantasize about, but how did we wind up at this point, alone, in the dark, bodies intertwined to the point of not knowing where one stops and the other begins? I'm still trying to figure it all out as I listen to her soft breathing, slowing as she nestles into my shoulder and starts to fall asleep. I could smell a scent of berries in her red curls, mixed with the raw smells of passion and sex that hangs in the air around us.

I could tell you how the night started, where it all began, but would you believe me, would you even care?

I know that the sun will rise soon, and I do not have very long to tell you my tale, but if you have the ear to listen and the mind to see, I will tell you.

The first rays of the sun are glinting in through the shades, off-white on cream-colored walls, the curtains are milky brown, almost like milk with a little bit of coffee in it, like her delicious flesh. I don't have to vanish because I am a vampire or some silly fantasy. I was meant to be paid for these hours last night, but with her, I felt something new, fulfillment.

My night had started off simple enough, dinner with an executive of some New York firm in town on business, nothing too fancy, just dinner and playing designated driver. She paid me for being there, simple as that. I had expected to be with her for the evening, but sometimes people just need company in strange cities. I tried to tell her, no, but she insisted on paying me for my services. I took it as a compliment, but I was feeling the weight of it all as I left her car in the garage under Market Square and walked across Summit Hill down to Market Square.

I had a pocket full of money from an easy night of work, a dirty feeling in my stomach and a desire not to be alone.

I strolled across the outdoor stage at the top of the Square like I owned the city, hiding my feelings inside behind an image of success and happiness.

The clubs and restaurants around me were alive with movement and music, drunken voices and live instruments. My ears were in tune with the pulse of the city, and I heard a voice, silky smooth, harmonizing with a single guitar, somewhere in one of the bars.

I let my ears do the driving as my feet followed, to the not so crowded entrance of Scruffy City Hall.

The guy checking IDs and collecting cover at the door recognized me as a regular and just waved me past, nodding as I went.

The poster in the window was black and white on classic tan cardboard, looking like the announcement pages of old, her name was Savory Clark.

In the image, her eyes were piercing but soft, her lips pouty and thick. I entered the hardwood and glass double doors to a nearly empty Scruffy, and the voice hit me full force.

She was in the back, on the stage, alone, with a crowd of about forty, moving and swaying to every single word. I was suddenly transported to another time in my mind, a place before this, when nothing was in front of me but life. She was working her way through a rendition of Charles and Eddie's Wounded Bird without trouble, her voice touching every note without missing a beat, her foot tapping the hardwood floor, keeping the beat with the piano.

Sitting there, rocking back and forth, alone on the stage, I could feel the electricity of the words coming out of her mouth, the emotion behind each syllable.

I'm not sure how many other songs she sang through, sitting there looking and sounding like an angel ready to take flight.

Being lost in the beauty of the music and the way it all made me feel.

When she stood to take a five-minute break, the crowd dissipated, and she slid through the crowd with grace and elegance, her thick booty and curvy hips swishing left and right to dodge random group members. Many of them shook her hand and told her how great she sounded, I exited to the bar and waited for her to make her way out of the crowd.

When she approached the bar, as luck would have it, a slot beside me was about the only one open, so this beautiful voiced goddess wound up directly beside me at the bar. I took this as a sign and cleared my throat.

"That was incredible," I said, waving the bartender, John, over to us. "What can I get you?"

"Um, I can get my drink thank you," she said in a voice that seemed to sound just as milky as her singing voice.

"No, please, let me," I pleaded with her. "I was having an awful night until I came in here and heard you singing."

"In that case," she said, a reddish tint filling her cheeks, "you can get me a bottled water for now. No need in falling before my set is over."

"Okay, my name is Sean," I said, offering a hand. She took it into hers, and my body was alight with sparks, electric energy flowed from her palm into mine.

"I'm Savory," she replied, grasping the bottle of water off the counter and turning back towards the back room and the stage.

"Can I get you a real drink after your set is finished?" I managed to get out before she was out of earshot.

"Yeah, if you can sit through another twenty minutes of Nina Simone and Leonard Cohen songs."

I sat at the bar nursing a glass of dark liquor as she made her way back to the stage, the drunken crowd cheered and she began singing a throaty version of "If It Be Your Will" by Leonard Cohen. She threw out names, expecting me to lose my interest.

I looked down at my phone and opened the playlist, every song she had sung, was there on the playlist. I waited the twenty minutes, which felt like an eternity as she sang one after another of the songs on my playlist as if destiny had intervened earlier in the night. When she went into her piano-only version of "Mississippi Goddamn," I moved around a little bit, a tap here and a twist there.

Savory ended her set with a charming and incredibly slowed down version of "Take My Breath Away" by Berlin that seemed to last forever, every moment as pleasurable to the ears as the one before.

She knew how to work for a crowd, as well, they were all dancing slowly, each couple embraced and even the single gentlemen and ladies, swooning to the soul of it all. Savory thanked the crowd for their support, bowed and gracefully walked down the steps in my direction.

"Have you ever been up to the rooftop bar," I asked her as I ordered myself whiskey in an iced-over glass and her a fruity drink that I had trouble pronouncing. She shook her head and let out a soft gasp as I led her up the wooden staircase that led out onto a rooftop patio that revealed the entirety of Market Square two stories below. The band behind her had finished setting up and began playing a mix of folk music and rock. I pulled out a chair for her at a table by the edge of the patio, and she sat in it, her curves working my eyes.

I sat across from her and allowed her the silence to take in the beauty of Market Square from above, the lights and the storefronts glowing in the darkness.

I just watched her as her eyes took it all in, her reactions and emotions to seeing it all from a brand new perspective. She slid a wooden tipped Black and Mild from a small purse and rolled the wrapped cigar in her hands before unwrapping it and placing it between her pouty lips, a hint of red lipstick staining the plastic. I brought out my lighter and held it out for her to light.

"So how did you like my set?" she asked, eyeing me to see if I was going to lie about her taste and quality of music. Instead of answering her, I slid my phone across the table and nodded at it.

"You tell me," I said, pointing at the phone and motioning for her to scroll through the playlist. She took a smooth puff from the cigar and exhaled softly while sliding down through the songs, her eyes getting wider for each song on the list.

"No way," she mumbled, taking a sip from the glass of vodka, tequila and some crazy blend of tropical fruits. "You must have downloaded these while I was singing."

"Actually, no," I said, taking my phone back and slipping it into the pocket of my grey, stonewashed jeans. "I was walking across the Square and heard your voice when someone was coming out of Scruffy, and I recognized the song."

"How about that, hmm?" she asked me, questioningly. "So why did you want to buy me a drink, Mister Sean? Or is this how you work for the crowd every weekend?"

"I don't know how to answer it just yet, or why," I replied, as honest as humanly possible, my palms starting to sweat. "I just heard something in your voice, that made me, that forced me to want to ensure I got to hear as much of it as possible."

"Ok, I can buy that," she replied, grinning. "But I hope you aren't expecting much from me, I've got a flight at seven a.m., and I'm on my way to New Orleans for a gig and an interview with one of the clubs down there for a full-time slot. The owners were here tonight, is why I was so short with you."

"I want nothing more than the time you are willing to share with me," I replied, finishing my drink and lighting a Kamel Red Smooth, my vapor pen left behind in the client's car by accident. "So what do you say we get out of here, walk around the city or something?"

"How do I know I can trust you?"

"You don't," I replied. "But you can."

******

As the minutes turned into hours, we talked about the downtown area of the city of Knoxville; I showed her things she never knew about the city she was raised in, hidden waterfalls and alleyways covered in graffiti. The look of wonder and amazement in her eyes reminded me of a time when the city was as mystical to me as Paris is to lovers. The stars tattooed on her left shoulder were moist with perspiration as we once again neared Market Square and I took a chance I was willing to risk. I pulled her close to me in the garden south of the square and kissed the stars, my tongue barely grazing her skin.

Savory gasped softly and shivered in my arms.

I felt the heat of her body through the loose and complimenting red lacy dress with straps so thin they shouldn't have even existed.

At that moment, I was pretty confident where the night would end, how the two of us would wake up, and for the first time in many years, I was scared. Scared that this woman before me would change something inside of me, make me want to change.

I am in the business of male prostitution to a higher class of women, business executives, authors, actresses in town for conventions and polite company.

Somebody could look at me and call me a prostitute or a ho, and they would be right.

That's just the honest truth of business I happened to fall into truth is, my number requires a couple of things to be acquired.

Someone couldn't just go onto the Back page and discover my name and picture.

My clients are all from the same class and circle of women, many of whom I do not even sleep with I escort them to dinner, a movie, we have a glass of wine, I bathe them, tuck them in and they go to sleep in my arms, then I leave. Some of them want more from me, and I oblige, but for the most part, I fill an emptiness in their lives of travel and business schedules, I give them the warmth of love and they pay me for it.

Savory held my hands in hers and kissed my fingertips, each one softer than the next, her lips moistening them, she laid her head on my shoulder, and we slowly swayed to the sound of the fountain behind us, the quiet splashes of the small waterfall.

I closed my eyes and moved with her in slow circles, our bodies moving as one.

I prayed to the God's of all beliefs and faiths that the moment would last an eternity.

But I knew it would not be. Eventually, the sun would rise, the dream would end. Eventually, the light that brings life to the day would burn the newly found soul out of me.

We strolled south out of the park and made a right, walking close, holding hands up the one-way avenue that would lead us to the walkway going across.

Gay Street and its many lanes of terror, there was a crosswalk, but the speed required to cross it, the energy required, neither of us wanted to waste it, so we chose the longer route.

Halfway down the avenue, I pulled her close and pushed her back against the wrought iron fence, surrounding a hidden parking lot, directly across from a late night coffee shop.

Savory moaned into my ear as I kissed her neck and shoulders again, nibbling at the stars on her flesh, like the mystical heroes of the stars.

She took one of my hands into hers and led it across the flesh of her thighs, the meat of her hips and against the cotton panties between, which I assumed would either be red or white, to match the tones of her lipstick, the glamour of her dress. I felt warmth and moisture soaking through, her essence moistening my fingers, even through the fabric. I kissed her lips for the first time and tasted the cigarillo she had taken puffs from through the night. She moaned into my mouth as I pressed against the fabric and parted her plump lips, moisture seeped through the material.

I brought my hand up, glistening in the moonlight and traced her lips with the juices and licked it away as fast.

She pulled my face to hers hard, our lips mashing, our teeth clicking against each other, it was rough and carnal, but it was delicious, and it was as elegant as anything I had ever seen in a film. I took a glance around and saw what I had hoped, the businesses were closed, the streets barren, a few lights in the condos above were open, but the street was ours. I held her face in my hands, kissed her lips, and she responded by pushing her body against me. I slid a hand across her breast, squeezing it gently as my hand traveled south down her side, her thigh, beneath the skirt again. I took her bare thigh in my hand and massaged the meat of her leg, the juiciness of it, arousing me more.

I slid her panties down her legs, my eyes locked into hers as I lowered myself, kissing her flesh as I inched them down lower, I expected her to stop me any moment, but she just moaned softly as I breathed on her through the dress.

Savory stepped out of the panties, and I tucked them into my pocket, I lifted the soft fabric to her waistline, looking one last time like a man about to cross the street, left then right, before kissing her thighs and spreading her lips, taking the edges of her labia into my mouth.

She moaned loudly as I pushed my tongue inside her labia, circling her clitoris like I was writing a poem in saliva.

She spread her legs wider to give me better access to her warmth, her fluids, her treasure.

I licked her lips and nibbled at her labia, enjoying each taste of her warm juice that met my tongue like an excited new neighbor.

I spread her lips wide, taking in the beauty of her fleshy pinkness before caressing her opening with my fingers, I pushed in with my index finger and watched built up juice flow down to my knuckle. I lifted my eyes and met hers as I sucked it from my finger and slid my tongue deep inside of her.

Savory moaned and grabbed the back of my shaved head, pulling me closer to her, I listened as she gasped for air, all of my senses awake, my flesh felt alive as I stroked the inside of her with my tongue.

The walls of her vagina came alive and massaged my tongue as I massaged her walls, my saliva mixing with the delicious juices of her body.

I pushed away and gasped for air before going back into the glorious salvation I was finding on a dirty street in my wretched city. She cried out, and I heard noises from above, but I did not care, I was invincible, dedicated, lost in the moment I was not sure if I would be able to find again.

A window opened above, a man yelling, a noise of something sailing through the air, a glass bottle busted mere inches away from where we stood.

I was up off of my knees in an instant, kissing her lips, feeling the heat from her cheeks. I took her hand in mine and led her away from the fence, determined to get across the crosswalk before the urges were too strong for us to control.

The intensity was raw and real inside of me, a beast craving to be let out. She kept up as we made it to the walkway and halfway across she pulled me close again, the wind blowing through the chain links cooling our hot skin.

Savory kissed me again, oblivious to the cars passing below, her body still shaking from the orgasm moments before against the fence. She kissed me hard, she kissed me deeply, as if she was trying to give her soul to me. I welcomed it, inhaled it, swallowed it down into my stomach and held it in my lungs until it burned, not wanting to let it escape my lips. Savory released me and exhaled sharply. I did my best to hold it in so that it would last a moment longer. But I had to let it out, so I did, feeling a bit of my heart breaking already.

"So, um, I have a room at the Holiday Inn, Sean, do you want to come with me?"

I looked at her as if she were mad, wondering why she felt the need to ask me that. I didn't understand, didn't understand at all. Suddenly I was confused. But I didn't even care; I wanted to be with her, even if she wasn't ever coming back to Knoxville. I wondered at that moment if everything would change in the morning if this were the moment where my road would fork. Savory's eyes were on me, a desire hidden inside them, beckoning to be let free. I met her gaze and smiled, a delicate and fragile smile, praying she couldn't see through the look in my eyes to the thoughts in my mind, the emotions in my heart.

"I'll go with you on one condition," I replied, kissing her lips again, sucking the bottom one and nibbling on her lip. She gasped and licked my lips, her hips grinding against me.

"What is it? What do you want? I'll do whatever it is you want?" she moaned through clenched teeth before kissing my lips again.

"I want you to stay tomorrow, don't go to New Orleans, stay here and figure out another way, or another time," I whispered, looking into her eyes and kissing her lips again. She shook her head and pulled away from me.

"I, I'm sorry, but I can't-do that," she began walking away, towards the end of the walkway, turning, starting to descend the steps. My mind was torn, my whole essence, torn at the seams, trying to decide if I should give pursuit or just walk away. I decided to follow my heart and give chase. I couldn't understand the emotions flowing through me; this is not what my body does. I am a male escort, a fucking prostitute; I help women fall in love for money, not fall in love with a stranger, only here for one night.

I stopped at the top of the stairs and watched as she rapidly crossed the street to the Holiday Inn, I lit a Kamel and fought the emotions inside of me. She looked back over her shoulder and up at me when she reached the other side. I wanted to yell out, to call her name, to run to her and pull her close, just to feel perfection again. But my voice was gone, my legs were like jelly as I stumbled down the two flights of ugly concrete steps. When I reached the bottom of the stairs, I looked up, and she was already gone. I ran across the deserted street towards the turning glass entrance, I tossed my cigarette away and went into the turnstile.

The doors were moving at what I assume is an average pace, but it felt like an eternity.

When the other side opened in the gap, I surged through, the cold air of the lobby's interior hitting me in the face, cooling the heat in my flesh.

My black Polo shirt was sticking to my back from the humidity outside, my grey jeans dirty at the knees.

I walked right to the counter, and the attendant was not impressed. His name was Ralph; he was dumpy, he had those triple thick glasses that make the eyes seem massive, his hair was long, black and always appeared oily. Ralph knew my occupation, knew my name and he was jealous of it all.

"What do you want, Sean?" he asked me, in that husky voice that put me into the mind of the killer in a slasher film. The man didn't even look up from his magazine, which I noticed at a glance contained naked women and various breeds of horses, I considered pointing this out as strange, but chose not to.

"I'm off the clock, Ralph," I told him, glancing at the digital readout of rooms beside him on the counter. "I'm just trying to return something to a guest of the hotel."

"A client earlier in the evening?" he asked, glancing up at me, sliding the readout beyond my line of sight under the counter.

"No, Ralphie," I replied, wanting to smack him and grab the tablet from his sweaty hands. "I just met her. She leaves in the morning, and it's already getting late. Can you please help me?"

"Sounds like a typical client to me," he said, turning his head back to his magazine. Blowing me off.

I fished out the wad of bills in my pocket and laid a crisp, new blue one hundred dollar bill on the counter. Ralph looked up at it, then at me, seeing I was serious. He reached out and palmed the bill, easing it into his pocket. His black slacks were strained at the waist and looking ready to lose a button at the first hint of another meal.

"What's the name? You know I can't give you the room number, but I can call up and see if she answers," he said, reaching for the house phone and the digital tablet.

"Savory Clark."

"Didn't she just come in a minute ago?"

"Yeah, I was right behind her, tying my shoe, and she dropped something on the walkway," I said, my hand feeling the cotton panties in my pocket, the moisture beginning to dry in the heat outside, now cold to the touch. Ralph dialed her room number and handed me the phone. I took it and waited, expecting her to ignore it and let it ring until the computerized operator answered.

"Hello," she replied, her voice warm and inviting as it had been at the bar, hours ago, what felt like a lifetime ago.

"I'm sorry, Savory, I am," I said, "I'm just nervous. I'm not used to feeling like this, especially, so suddenly. Can I please come up?"

"I need you to come up anyway; you have something of mine that I will need back. The room number is 913. Exit the elevator, turn left, and it's the second door on the right.

I need to go to the bathroom, so I'm going to leave it cracked, okay?"

"Okay, I'll be up there in a second. Thank you," I said, handing the phone back to Ralph and turning towards the elevators.

"Didn't sound like she dropped anything, Sean," he called after me.

"Oh, she did," I mumbled, "my soul."

******

As the elevator slowly rose to the ninth floor, I thought about everything that had transpired since she had finished singing, pondering what could have been so different, what could make me feel this way. I had not reached a conclusion when the ding sounded, letting me know I was at my destination. I exited the elevator and turned left, looking down the hall. The door was cracked directly ahead of me, beckoning for me to enter. All over again, my flesh was on fire; I was dizzy with the thoughts of holding her in my arms, pulling her close to me. I entered the door and closed it quietly behind me; darkness was my whole world. When my eyes adjusted, I noticed the lights outside the window, painting the room in a soft haze.

I looked around the room for Savory, and I could feel her presence.

From what seemed like the air, I felt her pressed against my back, her dress and bra, previously discarded, her hard nipples pressing into my back through my Polo shirt.

She pushed me against the window and kissed my neck, she slid her hands under my shirt, her fingers swirling in the bit of hair on my chest. She lifted my arms and pulled my shirt off, the chill of the air conditioner directly below me instantly cooling my hot flesh, her warm hands rubbing all over my bare skin as she kissed my back and neck, teasing me.

Savory grasped at the crotch of my jeans, squeezing, her flesh on my back, her nipples hard and thick, she kissed my neck and moaned into my ear.

I turned and met her naked beauty face to face, our heights seemingly the same. I kissed her delicious lips again and spun her like some erotic dance move, pressing her against the cold glass. I kissed her neck and held her breasts to my face, sucking on her nipples as gently as I could, flicking them with my tongue. She moaned again, this time, more elegantly, more dignified, more attached to the moment, now that we were alone, in the dark, until the sun rose.

I could feel her reaching for my belt, unlatching my jeans as I treated her breasts as gentle flowers that would break if my lips pulled even the slightest little bit.

My jeans fell to the floor, and she took me into her hand, she squeezed me, stroked me and felt what was there.

My thickness and length seemed to be approved as she tried to welcome me in right there, one leg lifted around my waist. I rubbed the head across her lips, watching in the almost darkness as the head pushed between her thick outer lips, leaving a smear of my undoubtedly shiny fluid on the delicate swollen flesh there.

I wanted this moment; I knew she did too, to press my way inside of her and feel her heat wash over me, to clutch me, to grasp me, so set me ablaze as our juices mixed, our two bodies became one, pressed against the darkened glass window.

I rubbed the head across her clitoris, recreating the circles I had made with my tongue, getting myself wet and I pressed into her, her vagina opening for me, grasping me. I could feel another orgasm about to rock through her body the way she clenched and released. Gasping, whispering my name and biting at my ear.

I felt it when it happened, the way she stiffened up against me, the juices, leaking down the sides of my shaft, burning through the cold air blowing up from the air conditioner. She let out a soft whimper and leaned against me, I lifted her face to mine, kissing her lips, massaging her face with my hands.

"I want you to come for me, Sean," she moaned out in barely a whisper. "You've earned it, come for me, Sean."

I eased out of her warmth and her welcoming, wet grasp, lifting her leg to the floor, she looked at me confused, almost hurt.

"Not yet," I said softly, "I will, just not yet."

I led her into the bathroom, flipping the switch, she turned away from the mirror, hiding in the crevice of my shoulder.

"What's wrong?" I asked, lifting her face to look at mine, her eyes meeting mine. "Don't turn away from it. It is you, it is beautiful, and I'm afraid, I'm falling in love with it, and with you."

Savory looked into my eyes and gave me a soft nod, nervousness in her beautiful eyes. She turned around facing the mirror, wrapping my arms around her waist, her thick booty, gyrating against my penis, the head, teasing the warmth coming from her vagina. I looked at her in the mirror, and I saw perfection, I saw the natural form of the goddess Aphrodite. She turned again to face me and kissed my lips, massaging me in her hands.

"Are you ready to come for me now?"

"Later, how about you run us a bath?" I replied, going into the other room for my phone.

As I bent to search for it, I heard the water begin to run in the tub; I glimpsed at the digital clock on the phone before sliding into my playlists. I picked a list consisting of many of the songs she had performed earlier, by their original artists and turned the volume down low, I switched the screensaver over to a burning candle and pressed play before closing the screen.

Savory was in the tub when I returned to the bathroom, closing the door and flipping off the light switch. I sat the phone on the toilet seat and let the sounds of Leonard Cohen fill the air. I eased into the tub behind her, the water steaming hot in the cold air. Savory moaned as I kissed her neck and snuggled back against me.

We talked about the past and the future as we took turns soaping up the rag and washing each other's bodies, while I did my best to dodge the employment question, at this point, prior work.

The hot soapy water relaxed us, calmed all of the heightened nerves in our bodies. When we had finished, as the water drained, we stood and took a hot shower, enjoying the feel of our bodies wrapped in one another. As the soap rinsed away, I felt as if the sins of my past, the crimes of my job washing away.

Savory slid down to her knees and took me into her mouth, letting the hot water mix with her saliva.

A fountain of heat that she plunged my penis in and out of, the feeling was sublime, and the urge to come for her was truly at a high point, I gently pulled her away and kissed her lips before turning off the water.

I carried my phone into the bedroom and sat it by the house phone on the bedside table, she untucked the blanket and slid between pure white sheets that seemed to glow in the candlelight from my phone's face.

I slipped between the sheets with her, and our lips met in the light of the sheets, the water on our skin chilling us as it evaporated from our bodies and smeared across the material we were wrapped in, I kissed Savory's lips again before vanishing under the sheets.

The radiant heat of her body was warming me as I proceeded to spread her vagina again with my face. This time was more passionate than the first, I buried my face between her lips and sent my tongue as deep inside her as possible, searching deep inside for her heart and soul.

Savory's orgasms came and went like the songs on the tablet, before I felt her hands under my armpits, gently urging me to join her above the covers. She kissed my lips, licked herself from my face and rolled me over onto my back; our thighs met as she slid me inside her warmth, her weight on me, her ass in my hands. At first, she rode me gently, finding a rhythm to the way I was moaning. When she found the perfect motion, she leaned back and grabbed my ankles, giving me the view of her face.

Her breasts were rising and falling as her breathing increased with mine, and her beautiful pussy, spread for me, a simple man inside her loving warmth, watching it rise and fall on my shaft, new streams of wet liquid running down it each time she would gasp.

Each time I felt her walls clench me and release. I expected her to stop and pull me on top of her, but she didn't, she slowly raised up and leaned forward. Our faces inched apart and kissed my lips, her hands in mine, grinding slowly against me, I could feel the throb and pulse, wondering if she could feel it too. The ache in me was tightening, begging for a sweet release inside this heavenly body of hers. I craved it as she asked me for it earlier.

"Are you ready, Sean?" she beckoned me, kissing my lips, a single tear rolling down her cheek and splashing across my mouth, I licked it and kissed her again.

I could feel it inside of me, ready to be out, ready to flow into the river that was her. I released her hands and clasped my hands behind her back, just above her waist, pulling her close to me, I squeezed her body tight to mine. I pulled her butt up and eased her down, showing her a slower pace. I grasped her back again and pulled her close as she kept with the rhythm of hands.

Savory inched her head up enough to kiss my lips with pecks, but also able to watch my eyes and my face. She nodded to me as another, more gentle orgasm rocked her body. As the squeezes took hold and released me, I released my everything into her, she pressed down onto me hard, grinding bone against bone, her pussy grabbed me, held me tight. Savory held me deep, the muscles inside of her, massaging me up and down, grasping, squeezing as the white milk of life left my body and entered hers.

Explosions in my mind, flashes behind my eyes, tears, began to pop up at their corners, Savory kissed them away, between moans and gasps.

"God damn, Sean," she cried softly. "I can't stop this. I can't turn it off."

I turned her face to mine and watched as she clenched her teeth, made the look again and shuddered atop me, another orgasm rocking her body, another round from me as well. We lay there like that for a long time, her shaking, both of us coming together like art, like magic. Eventually, the shakes subsided, and she rolled over to her side, facing away from me. I slid close beside her and kissed her neck, her ear.

Savory fell asleep clutched in my arms, the scents of our sex spread across the room, the bed, wet in some places, dry in others, our little haven from the world outside.

I glimpsed at that window and felt heartbroken as I can see the sun about to rise.

******

I eased out of bed as gently as I could, tiptoeing over to the window and looking out across the city, the sun slowly bathing the rooftops with life. The street below was quiet, a car here and there, driving slowly, trying to navigate the lanes and figure out the proper direction needed for forwarding motion. I ordered room service, a breakfast of fruits, juices, and coffee. I slid into my jeans and thumbed out another bill, meeting Rodney at the door. I knew Rodney as well as I knew Ralph, but Rodney was different.

Rodney, I had known for many years, before I wound up in this unique business of mine.

In school, we had frequented the same parties, sat at the same tables, conversed with the same people.

There was no jealousy in this man, and there was no twisted sense of self-worth with Rodney, he was like me, a human being, struggling to make ends meet in a fucked up economy.

"Hey, Sean," he said looking up from the food cart. "I didn't know you were here."

"I'm not here on business," I replied handing him the hundred dollar bill, with a forty dollar tip for the meal between us. I lifted the two trays like an expert server at the local Texas Roadhouse and retreated into the room.

"Catch me later in the day," he said, quietly. "I have a friend I want you to meet."

I let the door close on his statement as I eased back into the bed with the trays, setting them before Savory and gently kissing her lips.

She opened her eyes and saw me there, taking it all in, before attempting to snuggle back into the pillow.

"Hey, you can't go to sleep," I told her, you have to get down to New Orleans remember?"

Savory rose at the statement and looked around the room, nervous at the sight of the sun coming in through the window behind me.

"What time is it? I have to be out of here by six fifteen to make that flight," she replied, her eyes resting on the trays in front of us.

"It's fine," I said, lifting the silver lids, showing slices of mango, watermelon, grapefruit halves and glasses of orange juice, cups of black coffee, still steaming, on the edge of the trays.

"You have about thirty minutes before you have to be downstairs to make sure you catch the plane. I can go ahead and call your cab while you eat."

"But, I have to get ready, I have to be ready to go."

"Relax, eat, please eat," I said, reaching for the phone. I knew a couple of gypsy taxis in the area that worked even this early. Friends that would make sure she was on time, without swerving through the lanes, risking life and limb for a buck. "I know somebody that can get you there in twenty minutes tops."

She relaxed a little with the comment and ate a piece of the sliced mango with a fork, the sun through the window seemed to make her skin glow more, the tint in her hair shined in the rays of light. I was still in a mood of pure euphoria, and I didn't know when it was going to end.

"Hey, it's Sean, can you meet me downtown?"

"What's the fare."

"A lady friend, she's got to be at the airport by at least six forty-five."

"When does she want to leave?"

"I'd say, give us about thirty minutes to get up and all that."

"Oh, that kind of lady friend, man you must be rich," the voice on the other end laughed.

"Not that kind of party, Tony."

"Where yall at?"

"Just come to the convention center, the bottom of the walkway."

"I'll see you here in a few, and you better tip me well, Sean, it's early."

"Have I ever let you down," I replied, laughing as I hung up the phone.

I took my place beside Savory on the bed and munched on pieces of this and that, not tasting the fruits. Savory sipped on her glass of juice as I drank my coffee, the caffeine inside instantly bringing my senses back online.

"So how much do I owe you?" she asked me, her tone, flat and calculated, none of the warmth from last night. I already knew what she meant, but I tried to play around the question like any sane man would do.

"For breakfast, oh it's on me."

"Okay, Sean, we can stop playing romantic love story turned sexual adventure now, all right?"

"What are you talking about?" I asked her, the world built in the last seven hours collapsing around me, my own Pompei tragedy, destroyed by this woman's volcanic soul and sexuality. I suddenly felt played, I felt cheap, I felt dirty.

"I know who you are, and I am from around here, you know? I figured one of my friends put you up to this, as a send-off or something. So how much do I owe you?"

I pulled her close to me, the coffee cup forgotten and falling to the floor, shattering. I held her gaze and kissed her lips as hard as she had kissed me, harder even, I wanted her to feel what I felt, to understand this was no job, this was real.

Savory bit at my lips, drawing blood, before pulling away and gasping, panting, hot breath on my cold flesh. She looked confused, hurt, and lost.

"It wasn't for money, Savory," I said, standing, wiping my lips and proceeding to grab my various pieces of clothing from the floor, zipping my jeans.

I dug deep into my pocket, pulling free the cotton panties and running them through my fingers one last time. I tossed them in her direction and aimed for the door, not caring where they landed. "You're ride to the airport will be here in a couple of minutes, you heard where I told him to meet you. Don't worry about paying him; I'll pay him back later today."

"Wait, Sean," she called after me as the door closed, separating us again.

I stood in the hallway for a moment, sliding on black ankle socks, dark brown Rockports and my Polo, seeing if maybe she would attempt to follow.

After three minutes, she didn't, and I decided to walk to the elevator. I walked the thirty steps slowly, hoping to hear the door open behind me. I pushed the button, the elevator rose behind closed doors, as my heart sank behind ribs.

I stepped through the threshold of the elevator and felt the urge to turn back, to see her standing there, tears in her eyes, wanting me to come back, to return with her to the room, to hold her past the flight time, to have her follow me into my home. I saw what a whole future could be made of in that instant. I turned around as the doors closed, a hint of red flashed by the doors as they met in the middle.

******

I walked across the avenue and up the dirty concrete stairs to the walkway, slowly, hoping at some point I would hear her calling my name, telling me to wait. The call never came, my pace never slowed. I reached the other end of the walkway and sat on the steps, fishing in my pocket for the pack of Red Kamels, empty. How I felt at that moment, what a fucking metaphor, I thought to myself. I sat there for a moment, unraveling my earphones, searching on my phone for the right music to make me forget this time, erase this place, to just vanish.

I stood and began walking back towards Market Square, I plugged in my earphones, turned the volume on high and pressed play, the voice of Nina Simone flooding my ears, the melodies of Miles Davis making my flesh crawl.

I passed by the wrought iron fence, the busted bottle still laying there, millions of shards of glass it seemed like, another metaphor for my current emotional state. I was broken, I was not the same man I was last night, something in me had changed, someone had changed me. I had done something I don't usually do in my line of work.

I played a game of chance with my heart, and no matter how good I thought the odds, the house took my heart, the house won on a deck I thought I had rigged and ready for a full house, blackjack or snake eyes on the dice.

I had played against the house and lost the one thing I never truly felt like I had in the first place.

The Corner Market was closed, the whole street was closed. I turned my face to the sky and let out a yell. Not a scream, a roar of pain, of hurt, of suffering, of loss. I walked back across the way to the park, the garden of Market Square and sat on a bench.

I looked down at the concrete cracked and ugly; I closed my eyes, I began to cry.

I sat on that bench for what felt like hours, watching, waiting to see if she would stroll through the park in her silky red dress, but like life, it never happened.

When the Corner Market opened, I walked inside, nodding at the short Latina inside the island counter. I strolled the aisles, wiping at my eyes, searching, searching for something to take my mind off of her. It was too early for alcohol and energy drinks would just make my mind and heart race. I wanted something I would never find in this store.

I wanted to taste her lips again, feel her touch. I had a craving in my mouth to feel her flesh against my lips, to nibble at the stars on her shoulder. I picked up a package of chips and skimmed over the nutritional facts, pretending I cared. I stood by the vegetables and weighed them in my hands, my mind on cooking, and Savory. I walked back up to the register with a selection of potatoes, a head of lettuce and a few green peppers.

Everything I touched, I pictured her in my hands, I craved to be in her presence. I made it to the register and noticed Gloria still staring at me. I lifted a hand to my eyes, but they were dry. I slid my items onto the counter and took in Gloria as she rang up everything. Four foot nine, maybe, almond-colored eyes, and wide shoulders. She looked like the type of girl that would go out for football in high school. Just to prove a point, she would try out for the team.

"So, Sean, what's the chef's masterpiece tonight?" She inquired while weighing the various vegetables.

"I'm not sure yet," I replied, my mind racing, I wanted to be out of this place, out on the street. "Can you throw a pack of Black And Milds with the wood tip in the bag also?'

"Not your regular Kamels?" she asked me, bending to reach the cigarillos, showing a booty in tight black slacks that would make some men do anything to possess it.

"Yeah, give me a pack of those too," I said turning my attention away from her assets and reaching for the cash in my pocket. The bills were there. I had imagined the panties still being there as well. Then I remembered throwing them at her in the room, before my dramatic departure. I regretted it all at that point, I should have sat back down, talked to her, told her how I felt inside.

Gloria returned to the register and beeped the two packs before tossing them into the bag.

She wasn't giving me shit about my smoking today.

She could tell something was wrong with me, everybody around could tell something was wrong with me, I knew it, I could feel it in my bones.

"Twenty-four, seventy-six," she said, handout, still looking up at my face as if a sign was there saying something like "HUG ME."

I handed her two twenties, and when she gave me my change, I shot out the door like a bullet.

No location was on my mind, specifically. I was just walking, walking with no direction, while the bag in my hand got heavier and heavier like the weight on my shoulder.

I strolled through downtown, walked over into the Old City and sat in Old City Java, nursing a cup of strong Irish Coffee, the daily blend, reading the Metro Pulse.

The paper filled my mind with local stories and situations needing resolutions around the city. I needed to be free of the imagery in my head, the feeling of her fingertips on my skin. I drank another cup and cut down the alley between Java and the pizza joint, the walls, once decorated with beautiful graffiti, now covered with the same bland cream color.

I took in the back alley and remembered moments in time spent there, clouds of marijuana smoke from my younger days, bottles of liquor in paper bags between sets, local bands playing their hearts out to coffee-fueled teenagers in pubescent heat.

I loosened one of the cigarillos the way she had, rolling it between my fingers, listening to the wrap crinkle as I worked my hands slowly in circles. I released the cellophane into the breeze and put the tip to my lips.

The taste of the tip, even before I lit the cigar, was like a piece of Heaven, a wash of relief in the already warm morning air. Humidity clung to me like dew on the grass, and in my mind, I was as cool as a cucumber. But when I took the first inhale as the lighter met with the tobacco, I was embraced by a cool breeze in the hot, muggy air. As if a spirit had wrapped me up and held me for an instant before disappearing into the sky. I collapsed to my knees, gasping for breath, not wanting the moment to pass. The cigarillo was falling away from my hand, me grasping for it.

I hit it again and could taste the promises on her lips, the desire in her flesh.

The hint of smoke on sweaty flesh. I knew the moment were lost and I tried to regain my composure before leaving the alley, beginning my short trek home. At least for a moment, I felt alive, able to get something done today. So, I strolled across the street, pulled out my keys and unlocked the old fashioned wood on glass door next to the cigar shop. The interior of the hallway is just like the Old City, old and fragile as if one step will send you plummeting through the stairs into whatever hole is beneath. Every step is worn and faded, splinters on edges, the rest, smooth to a touch of age. A creak follows every drop of the foot, the walls are of faded blue plaster, peeling in some places, non-existent in others.

The door at the top of the stairs, redwood with tan trim, is the entrance to my kingdom, my little hell on earth.

I live there, I exist there, and I walk into my kingdom alone, a broken man.

The studio apartment was that way because I had decided to have it that way. I had ripped out the thin paper walls on all of the little rooms, except the bathroom and made one large room with a small glass square in the corner. I never brought work home with me, and I never met work in front of the doorway.

I sat the bag of groceries on the kitchen counter, black imitation marble with faded caulking, and walked across the room to the stereo, a simple two speaker system with a five-disc changer and two cassette decks.

I wanted to go over to Broadway, swim in the tape collection at The Other Record Shop, but my heart wasn't in it. I fished around in the cassettes stacked against the wall and found the one I was looking for, I slid the tape out of its case and into the deck, pressing play.

My system is set up to amplify the tribble and catch the bass, to push it through slowly instead of a continuous thump, thump, thump.

The sounds of Miles Davis filled the room. I took a shower in scalding hot water, my tears seeming to be even hotter. As Miles painted Sketches of Spain around me in audio, I rinsed off and let myself air dry as I sliced up the vegetables and brought a pot of water to a boil. I evenly portioned two cups of rice and boiled the water for it separately. The waters boiled, and my eyes ran, the steam cleansing me of my thoughts for a few moments.

I pulled a large bag of crawfish from the freezer and portioned out a pound, sealing the bag and placing it back in the freezer, the craw's in a large mixing bowl soaking in rum and butter. When the larger of two pots came to a boil, I dumped in the vegetables and added a cup of seasoning I had mixed myself. A cup of sea salt, a spoonful of lemon pepper, Irish seasoning and a twist of dried peppers to give it a little kick. The smaller pot began to boil, and I tossed in the two cups of rice and a sprinkle of sugar to work with the flavors. By the time the cassette was ready to flip, the vegetables had softened, and the rice had been drained and fluffed.

I drained the crawfish bowl and placed them in a silver strainer it looks like a noodle strainer, but you can put it into a tall pot over boiling water.

So your selected items steam instead of cook in the boiling water, setting it gently into the tall pot and covering it all with a lid. I spread the rice in a large bowl and set a healthy chunk of butter on top to melt through as I finished the other ingredients. I could feel my mood changing, each second I spent stirring this and seasoning that. The pain was fading, the images melting in my mind, held by a silken thread at the back of my mind, waiting to burst forward at a hint of her.

I switched the cassette for the original score of Risky Business, deep melodramatic instrumentals with vocalized songs few and far between, I was feeling better as the day faded, my energy returning.

I grabbed my phone from the counter and decided to call a friend. I was feeling better, but I couldn't go back to work like this. And, work, what the fuck was going on there? I slept with women and made them feel loved and wanted for a living, but falling in love, it just seemed like an improbability to me. Why was I so hard up for this woman? Where was the sense in this senseless world anyway?

******

Affair Of The Heart

(Six Months Ago)

It was a Friday night, late, slower than usual for a businessman like myself. I was in my apartment overlooking the Old City, sipping a glass of Remi Poujol's Le Temps Fait Tout, imported from Paris by a friend of mine who owns a liquor store and cigar shop in the middle of downtown. I had the windows open, the smells of the pizza joint across the way, more faint than usual due to the misty kind of rain hanging in the air outside. I was stretched out on the couch, leisurely, smoking a Marlboro 72 light, my brand of the month, and enjoying the breeze in a pair of Hanes all-cotton boxer briefs, blue with red stitching, when the phone rang. I checked the screen ID before answering, Chuck, another cab driver for the airport on the other end, probably with a job offer.

"Chuck, how are you doing, man?"

"Sean, brother, you busy, my friend?"

"Unless you count sipping wine and counting flowers on the wall as busy, no sir."

"I just dropped a lady off, Market Square, she's here for the conference tomorrow. Asked if I knew any nice gentlemen around town. Of course, I lied and said I knew one. You interested?"

"You at least get a name before you pimped me out, Chuck?"

"Yeah, brother, get this. Her name is Hart, Cynthia Hart. Is that fucking kismet or what, Sean?"

I could hear him laughing through the phone at his joke.

Little fat bastard, he always led the good paying women and good looking women my way. Of course, we had to rib each other once in a while. A couple of times, I even offered to put him in the game with some of my less specific clients. But Chuck was married, happily married, no. But married none the less, he cursed like a sailor and drank away most of his fare, but marriage meant something to him. The man had true values. I respected him for it, and I always cut him in on the profits.

"What does she look like? She's not gonna be at some dive on Cumberland, throwing back beer and slaw dogs is she?"

"Hell no, brother. This girl is an angel! Absolute fucking doll."

"I'm listening," I said, getting interested, finally sitting up and considering getting dressed while downing my glass of wine. No way I was going to waste good wine. And he said Market Square so that I could walk to my destination, shit; I could crawl if it came down to it. I gave him my undivided attention. "Come on, Chuck, speak!"

"She's your type, my man. Skin like molasses, beautiful round breasts, a little bit of a tummy.

The kind you could hold onto and... Oh sorry.

Hair's short, in a kind-of bob. These dimples when she talks, I tried to keep my eyes on the road, it was hard, man.

But her eyes, she had some silver eyeshadow, which made them, I don't know, almost glow. They hung low like she'd been smoking, you know I offered her a bag of fireweed. She said she didn't smoke. She has natural bedroom eyes. I mean, when she paid me and asked me about a male friend. I was speechless, got lost in there for a second." I could hear the strain in his voice describing this woman to me. I had faith in Chuck, and his descriptions were never off.

"Where'd you pick her up at?" I asked while standing and walking across the room to the hall closet, where I kept my one nice suit, dry cleaned weekly, even if I hadn't been out. Wrapped in plastic and a suit bag, at all times. This thing was immaculate. It had cost me a couple of grand, and worth every penny.

"Crown Plaza," he replied. "Saw her keycard when she started to pay me. She's staying in the penthouse, man. For a four-day conference. The fucking penthouse."

I listened, slightly intrigued. I pulled the suit bag off the hanger and unzipped it, smelling the cleaners detergent through the plastic bag. "She's got red highlights in her hair and a blood red dress. Man, she;s fucking beautiful."

"Okay, you got me," I replied, tearing the plastic off the suit. "Where's she going to be at?"

"Should be strolling around Market Square," Chuck laughed, "she didn't realize all she had to do was walk across the street and down some steps. I'm quite certain. Or maybe she just wanted a stranger and not someone from the hotel, to ask for some company."

"Did she leave a number?" I asked running a lint roller over the immaculate suit before me; I didn't even want to put it on, it was so dapper. I knew a guy, that knew a guy, and got it way under price. But the stitching alone let people know where it had come from and made people stop mid-conversation to admire its beauty.

"Yeah," he replied, "you got a pen?"

"Chuck, give me the number and get off the damn phone. I trust you, okay?"

Chuck gave me the number followed by an excellent line of profanities that men who share bonds are known to pass back and forth in a joking tone, then hung up.

A ray of light from the streetlamp outside my living room window blazed across the room, giving the suit an angelic glow.

Designed and tailored by the one and only John Reyle, the suit was a one of a kind. A black suit top, with red inseams, gray stitching and only one pocket on the outside.

The inside was loose, an inner right pocket high on the chest, the material a silky red, the pants were more of the same, but with two front pockets and one on the back, left.

A red Louis Vuitton tie with seven silver lines going horizontal hung around the neck of the hanger, tucked inside was an officially branded one of a kind Armani white knit dress shirt, twelve buttons, all black, sparkled in the light of the streetlamp.

I kept a nice pair of shoes, polished and tucked away, for the special occasions. I chose to wear the piece of artwork before me out in public, compared to the suit, the top cap Ralph Lauren black dress shoes were shabby, even with a glow of polish that I could breathe on and wipe away a smudge.

I walked down the steps, dodging the one that always creaked so loud I would grit my teeth.

I opened the green door and was in the Old City, and my night had begun, a job was underway.

Honestly, I felt alive, like Lestat walking through the streets of New Orleans in the 80s.

I was ready, and I was focused. I would find my prey, make her forget about her problems at home, her job, her flaws, whatever they may be.

I would seduce this woman like she was a regular lover, not someone paying for my services. The way Chuck described her, I had a hard time believing picking a man up would be very hard. This woman sounded gorgeous, and I wanted to find out.

I was about to walk in the rain before I realized the trolley ran late on Fridays in the summer. The Green Line would get me where I needed to be in a matter of minutes. Besides, I wanted to stand out in front of Hannah's and let the ladies inside see me, their men sick with envy. I was dressed to kill like a James Bond movie, and I was feeling the energy. I felt like I had snorted a line before leaving the loft, but knew otherwise.

The trolley arrived just as a homeless man in dirty rags he liked to consider clothes and bedding were asking for a cigarette, I gave him two. What can I say?

I was feeling too good for everything to go right tonight, I could feel it, down in my bones.

I rode the trolley as far as Locust before I made a hasty exit, there was a stench onboard, a mix of piss and pure grain alcohol that made my stomach churn.

I never really used cologne, but if I had that odor would have eaten it away in minutes. I walked up the avenue, glimpsing to my left.

An iron fence around a large parking lot sat there; I wondered what building had been torn away to make this monstrosity, one day, I'd leave a more positive mark on the lot, christening it for the building lost so more urbanites could park in my part of town. I lit a cigarette and slowed my stroll down to a brisk walk, eyeing the park ahead. I wondered if she would be there, staring into the pond at the parks bottom, reflections of the stars making her eyes sparkle.

I caught a familiar chill walking through the small park towards the lower end of Market Square. The thrill of the hunt, even if it's a guarantee, always gave me a chill, butterflies in the stomach.

I could feel my balls tightening at the idea of spending the night with a woman of class, of elegance. I mean, there were women around, that weren't tricks, that were friends and I loved them, but the scent of sex with a woman of my caliber wasn't allowed to believe existed, that does something to me, something hard to explain.

The sounds of a Friday night on the Square hit me before I even stepped up onto the Square proper sidewalk. Live music this way, hot food that way, alcohol mixed in with all of it. I glimpsed around, halfway expecting I'd have to hunt for her, kill the romance by calling her cellular phone and asking directions, but I was wrong. The short stage where they put on Shakespeare in the Summer, at the top of the Square, she stood leaning against one of the four support beams, watching the lights sparkle through the fountains on the TVA steps. And Chuck was right; she looked like the Devil in a Red Dress, or an Angel in Red, whichever you prefer. Even from a distance, I could see the little silver lines above her eyes, the pronounced curves in her thighs, hips, and breasts. She didn't just look beautiful; she looked delicious like a red apple fresh off of the tree.

I tossed the cigarette away and stopped at a water fountain, rinsing off my fingers and gargling a little bit of it in my mouth, Chuck didn't tell me if she was a smoker or not.

I was suddenly nervous as I got closer to her, less than ten steps away, softly from one of the clubs, I heard a song I knew well, "Night Calls" by the recently deceased Joe Cocker.

I stood there a moment, admiring her body, the curves, the angles, the way the dress cried out to be peeled away from her chocolate flesh. I tapped my foot to the rhythm as I realized it must be 80s night at one of the joints close by, most likely Preservation Pub, I would do my best to convince her to go there with me, as soon as I spoke to her. I whispered her name under my breath, twice before I managed to say it loud enough for her to hear me.

"Cynthia?" I asked, she turned again, and our eyes met. The street lights are playing tricks on the silver lines above her eyes. I could sense a hurt buried inside her somewhere.

I noticed the diamond ring on her wedding finger, but being a gentleman of the night, chose not to speak on it.

What she does back home, is none of my business, I'm paid for the here and now, was my mentality, even if only for a little while. She stepped down the two steps, slowly, calculated. I could tell she had been drinking as well. The smell on her breath escaped me, but when she spoke my name, I knew it wasn't anything from the bars around here. The wine on her breath was too fancy for these joints. I couldn't name the brand, but I knew it was probably stashed up in her hotel room.

"Sean?" she said, shyly. She squeezed her arms together causing her breasts to bulge at the top of her dress. "You are Chuck's friend, right?"

"Yes, ma'am," I replied, taking her left arm on my right and leading her in the general direction of Preservation Pub. "Have you eaten?"

"Yeah, I ordered at the hotel before I called Chuck. Some little Japanese place that delivered. Sushi and spring rolls. A small bottle of Sake'. Do you like Sake', Sean?"

"When it's cold, I don't drink the warm stuff much. What's the other smell on your breath though?" I asked, intrigued. "It's wine, but I can tell it's not local. It smells great."

Cynthia breathed into her hand and giggled. She did the same and brought the perfume of the wine caught in her hand up to my face. I inhaled deeply, taking in the scent of the wine and the smells of her flesh behind it. The body lotion was expensive, too. Dolce and Gabanna if I had to take a guess, a blend of honey was in there somewhere, I would assume it was with the spring rolls. I couldn't smell the foods on her breath, she had cleaned up before coming out, but the wine had come after.

"I still don't know," I honestly replied, holding open the door to the Pub for her, guiding her up the stairs to the second floor and tables with candlelight.

"It's an orange Pet-Nat I forget the brand; my husband brought it back from France last year. He's been pretty frigid since. I knew I had a conference coming up, so I stole his treasured bottle of wine and drank the whole bottle over delivery sushi. I'm sorry, I'm sure you don't want to hear this," she mutters rapidly as I ease out a chair for her to sit across from me, the music downstairs, vibrating through the floor, sending tingles through my chair, through my body. I know she feels it too.

"Oh, I don't mind," I reply, giving her a typical devilish grin, but she's buzzed, so it does the trick. She truly is stunning to look at, the lines in her forehead, marks of beauty and the work she has put in to get where she is in this world of industry and commercialism. The silver above her eyes plays tricks in the candlelight, making shadows dance across her eyebrows every time she turns her head. "Tell me more about you, instead of him, I mean unless you want to talk about him all night, I'm sure your room has the pullout couch. I am also a licensed shrink, you know?"

Cynthia laughs, and it warms me, feels good deep inside. One of the bartenders that knows me knows my occupation, makes her way to the table and asks what all we'll be having.

I order a full bottle of good aged Jack Daniels bourbon and two glasses, a small bucket of ice, a bowl of fried pickles and she takes leave. Yeah, fried pickles aren't on the menu, but I tip well, and some of the bartenders owe me more than they can ever repay in fried pickles. Cynthia smiles at the way I handled our order, taking control, laying it all on the table. She reaches under the table and squeezes my thigh, purring quietly.

"I love that suit," she says, her hand massaging my thigh under the table, my hardness, teasing the sides of her fingers. "How, may I ask, did you get one of those suits all the way in Knoxville, Tennessee?"

"Oh, you recognize it," I reply, actually aroused more at the fact she knows who made my suit. "Are you a Reyle fan?"

"My husband owns three," she replies, squeezing at my penis, gauging the girth, knowing from where her hand is on my thigh, I can capture the depth quickly. She cups the edge of the head, massaging it through the material, through my boxers. I moan quietly as the bartender returns. Her hand doesn't leave my thigh.

"Sean, might I recommend the rooftop, it's closed due to the rain, but I'm sure Charles wouldn't mind if you were up there," she asks, noticing Cynthia's hand, but not acknowledging it.

I not and we stand, following her around a smaller stage and up a long steep flight of wooden stairs.

The stiffness in my pants, held in place by two layers of fabric, Cynthia is ahead of me, her skirt rising as we climb the stairs, I believe on purpose.

I see thick chocolate thighs that climb into the dress, a round firm and bare ass greet me as we near the top of the stairs. Cynthia stops suddenly pretending to trip, my face finds its way between her cheeks, feeling the heat, smelling sex and another expensive fragrance. Before the bartender notices, she is walking again, looking over her shoulder, grinning. I let out a soft sigh as they reach the rooftop doorway.

I light up a cigarette and just stand there, listening to the bartender escort Cynthia to a table near the edge of the building, overlooking Market Square. Cynthia seems pleased with the view, the bartender returns to the door, smiling, and waves me past her.

As she descends the steps, I rise, exiting onto the roof, the misty rains have stopped, a light fog in the air.

It blankets us from the Square below, just coming alive.

Cynthia is leaned against the edge, her dress, blowing sideways in the breeze, exposing her round booty and small vagina.

The labia too is chocolate colored, but the walls, are a bright pink and look moist even from a distance. I stand beside her, looking down at the crowd, imagining the taste of her pussy, the warmth of it on my face. Cynthia leads one of my hands to her crotch, using my fingers to rub it up and down, I can feel her clit hardening, her juices starting to run. She looks at me and smiles, her other hand finding my hardness again. I had expected to make it to the hotel, but it seems Cynthia wants something else, something hard, fast and rushed. I am tempted to tease her, drag it on as long as possible, please her in more ways than one.

Cynthia releases my hand and my penis at the same time; I massage her clit as she pours both of us a shot and lights one of my cigarettes.

We throw back the drinks, and she inserts my fingers into my mouth, a sensation of bliss as I taste her juices behind the hard liquor.

Sweet and sticky, the juices that leak from her pink fountain.

I have the urge to suck her pussy right then, to make her cry out to the crowds below, to come on my face, to beg for me to ram myself inside her until she comes again and again, but I resist. I want to see what she has in mind.

"Does that taste good to you, daddy?" she purrs, pouring two more shots, this time, rubbing her clit and smearing the juice along the rim of my glass.

"If I said no, I'd be a liar," I reply, taking the glass from her, licking the side and downing the shot.

Cynthia's juices mixed with the liquor excited me more. I had the feeling whatever I was feeling earlier was beginning to transpire, as if she were the one being paid to satisfy me.

But who was I to say no, so I went with it, decided to let this road lead us where it may.

I took the cigarette from her lips and took a long drag, she sat in one of the chairs, elbows on the edge of the roof and as if nothing had just happened began talking, about herself, about her husband.

It was a strange turn of events, but I listened. I took the chair beside her and moved it so I could sit as close to her as possible, wrapping an arm around her as she gave me her life's tale.

Cynthia laid her head on my shoulder and started at the beginning.

They had been high school sweethearts in New York, swearing to be together forever. Cynthia had taken his promises to heart and had thought he had as well. The first few years were rough, colleges in different states, weekends together few and far between, after college, they were together again, inseparable. He continued to pursue a Bachelor's degree while she worked day and night at a firm for the rights of mentally handicapped youth. He graduated and went to Wall Street, becoming a fund manager in under a year, she became a partner within three.

They were happy, or so she thought, he had long hours watching the market, talking to companies whose stocks were under his control.

Trips to other states and countries became routine, a monthly thing, then a weekly thing until he was hardly at home at all. Cynthia had always been faithful to her husband, kept the house clean no matter her hours, cooked when he was in town, on Skype when he wasn't. But she had her suspicions. And last year after France, he came back, distant and cold. At that point, she started sobbing into my neck, telling me about the lipstick on his white shirts, the perfume on his slacks.

I shushed her with an index finger to the lips and kissed them, then I kissed the tears and whispered in her ear, "I'll always be here for you, Cynthia."

She moaned softly and kissed me back, hard. Our teeth met with a soft clink and spread for our tongues to find access in a different mouth.

I kissed her soft and slow, nibbling on her bottom lip and licking her neck with the tip of my tongue.

She rose from her chair and sat in my lap, her warmth filling my crotch, causing me to moan with desire. She wiggled her shoulders as she kissed me, her dress sliding down around her breasts, large, lovely nipples greeted me as she poured drops of Jack onto her tits and pulled my face in close to suckle the liquor from her firm flesh. I obliged and switched back and forth between the two, then she squeezed them together, and I had both in my mouth at the same time. My slacks felt wet and hot as she rubbed her crotch back and forth across my shaft through my clothes. I felt a hand reach down and grasp at my pants, freeing the button and expertly unzipping them. I lifted her up, gripping her ass tight as she slid my pants and boxers down, my hardness, rubbing against her opening for the first time.

Cynthia was ready well before the moment, she guided me into her tight warmth, trying to find an angle to take more of me into her body. I sat back down and moaned aloud as I entered her fully, pushing past her lips and labia, deep inside her warm pink opening. Her juices ran down my shaft, warming my balls and making them sticky. The sensation was one I would remember forever, but something still felt off. I pushed her up off of me, the air feeling cold on my moist and wet shaft, I tucked it into my pants and zipped up, while she stared at me, mouth agape.

"The fuck is this shit, sir," she yelled at me, adjusting her dress, ignoring the little lines of liquid running down her thighs. "I'm paying you for a service, and you are not fulfilling your part of this bargain."

"What's going on here," I replied, lighting a cigarette and inhaling hard. I was confused, and I wanted answers. If I had to walk away from the money, I would walk away from the money. No harm, no foul, no need to be paid.

"What do you mean? He cheated on me repeatedly, and now he won't sleep with me! I'm out of town with a get fucked for free, well, not free, card and that's what I thought was happening right here!"

"There's more to it than that," I said, eyeing her reaction, gauging her demeanor. "I can feel it; it's more than that. This isn't the first time you've done this. There was no shyness, no hesitation. Talk to me, or I walk, simple as that."

Cynthia hesitated, trying to muster a smile, trying to step closer, reaching out. I backed away and stood my ground, feeling like an asshole, but knowing it was required. The desire to finish what we had started was strong, but the desire to know was much stronger.

"Why can't we just fuck and be done with it, Sean?" she asked, again reaching for me. "Tell me that first and I'll answer your questions."

"Because that's not the way I work," I replied, "I know something is up and I'm not going to take part in your game, whatever it is. Sex and romance are fine and dandy, but something else is going on."

"He's here, too," she replied. "Somewhere in this city, doing the same thing I am, with some other woman.

I know he is because he told me. And the son of a bitch thinks I'm just going to take it. I'm doing this to prove a point, and if he doesn't get the point, I'm filing for divorce when we get back to the city. Simple as that."

At this point, she had started sobbing again, I finally gave in and let her grab me this time, her face burying itself into my neck. Her warm tears running down the neck of my suit, absorbing into the fabric at my stomach line, somewhere. I honestly didn't know how to continue at the revelation. I was as confused as this woman, my employer of the evening. I felt like shit for dragging it out of her, but the chill was gone, my shoulders had relaxed, I exhaled.

I lifted her chin and met her eyes with mine.

"Hey, Cynthia," I said, softly. "It's okay; you can make it through this."

I tossed a hundred dollar bill on the table, grabbed the bottle of Jack, and led her away towards the door downstairs. I wasn't sure at how much time had passed; the Jack was talking to me, making things soft, plush, the world had a warm fuzzy tint to it. When I opened the door, I let Cynthia step through in front of me; the liquor was affecting her as well. Every step she took was slow, calculated. At the same time, she was wiping at her eyes, I followed slowly, not as far gone as she was, but feeling the booze, none the less. We made it to the bottom after what seemed like an eternity, shuffling around on the second floor. I took her hand and led her down the curved steps to the first floor; the music was quiet, the crowd hushed. The night was nearing its end.

I led her to the dance floor and pulled her close, the music playing mellow and soft. The song playing was a sweet version of Guns N Roses "Don't Cry," the voice female, the cords and riffs, bluesy and slow instead of the original hard rock love ballad mix. I held Cynthia close and looked into her eyes, smiling softly.

"It'll be okay," I whispered in her ear as the song ended, we spun slowly, nothing fancy, her arms around my shoulders, my hands on her hips.

The DJ spinning said the name of the artist who had sung the rendition, Savory or Savory, something of the sort, and dropped in a promotion that she would be singing live at Scruffy City Hall in a few short weeks.

I had never heard of her but had the urge to do some research. I would forget the name by morning, liquor fueling the night before. Cynthia sighed and pulled me away from the dance floor, leading me outside. The rain had picked up again, soft and misty, a cool breeze hanging ever close.

I held Cynthia close to me and led her away from the Pub, up the square and past the stage she had been standing on, we strolled across Wall Street and watched the little fountains in front of the TVA sign before proceeding up the steps.

"Where are we going?" she asked, looking around as I led her up the grey layered steps leading to the open patio between the two tall TVA buildings, Cynthia looked up, realizing how close she had been to the Crown Plaza, she giggled. "Oh, um, yeah, we're not going in there."

"Why not?" I replied, smirking. "Isn't this where you're staying, you want revenge. Why not leave it all over the sheets for him to find?"

"I, I can't-do that," she answered, looking down at the ground. She looked up at me, expecting a solution to all of her problems at home, a way out of everything wrong in her marriage.

I urged her on, taking baby steps to the crosswalk that would lead us over to the Plaza and into the main lobby. At first, she resisted, then slowly, she stood close to me, stiffened her back and held my hand. I was known here, a man of the night, an elegant expense for beautiful women. The late-night skeleton crew would know what was going on, would keep quiet.

The business at hand had changed from pure seduction and sex to a game of cat and mouse, a plot thick with holes that were yearning to be filled.

I would carry out my obligation for money, but more so, for the satisfaction that after this point, she would be a woman freed. I love my job, I love the women I meet and have sex too, but more so, I love their freedom and individuality, and her life at home was destroying her, piece by piece by piece. I wasn't entirely comfortable with the situational hazards here, the possible return of the cheating asshole mid-thrust, but maybe that's what she needed to be free of him.

As we walked past the closed bar and the elegant staircase toward the elevator, it gnawed at my stomach like the burn from that first shot of hard liquor, the cheap shit and how it made the belly boil. Cynthia apparently loved this man with all of her heart, from what I could tell, had been with no other men, while he had spread their sacred gift with women across the country, possibly the globe.

She had dedicated her life to him at an age unheard of in today's sexual and marital climates. Her love for him warmed my heart, but his complete disregard fueled my anger. She leaned over and gave me a nervous peck on the cheek while we stood waiting for the elevator. She giggled again, smiling.

"I feel like I did on prom night, the first time David and I had sex," she was blushing as she spoke. I could see a sparkle returning to her eye. Women are such sensual creatures, the simplest of behaviors can make their lives magical. I could feel it radiating off of her.

"Do you want me to be him?" I asked, as we walked into the elevator. "Should I treat this like our first times? Gentle and slow, but over in two minutes?"

This time I got a horse laugh out of her as she pushed the top floor button, Chuck was right, classic rich lady.

"No," she replied, losing some of the glow. "Just be you, Sean. Just do what you would do any other time."

She came to me as the elevator rose, kissing my lips softly, holding me close. I held her tight in my arms and spread her lips with my tongue, gently licking at the tip of hers. We shared a moment there before the elevator came to a stop, our bodies sober, our senses aware and awake. The doors to the elevator opened on the top floor, and we separated. Standing there in the hallway was her husband, back to us, tie in his hand, slightly hunched, apparently drunk.

Cynthia shoved me back into the elevator as the doors began to close and motioned with her hand to call her. I waved and smiled and descended in the elevator.

******

The night was ending, and I had not been paid, had not fully done my job. But I was satisfied that I would see her again, tomorrow. Cynthia was one of those women that pursued what she wanted, fed her desires, maybe not sexually until now, but otherwise. I'd call her in the afternoon and begin where we had left off. As I exited the Plaza, I glanced up at the top floor windows, all of the lights were on. I noticed a tied fly against the glass and then a bottle of liquor. It was heavy, thick glass, so the bottle busted and ran down the inside, not affecting the window at all. There was no way to tell where the argument was going, so I took a left and started the seven-minute walk back to the loft. Down Summit Hill, across Gay Street and past the strange red piece of modern art that looked like a penis twisted around a stick.

I caught a glimpse of tail lights twice walking down the sidewalk, and both times, bright red tail lights, with a flickering blue license plate light.

I shook it off as nothing and continued my little walk to the green door and my loft, uneventful. The streets were quiet, the breeze was cooling, and the sky was clear. The interstate was even calm, not a thousand yards from the loft, cars zipping by quietly in the night. When I got near the door, I noticed a car pacing by, a black Nissan Maxima, I couldn't see through the tinted windows, but when it passed, the same bright red tail lights and same flickering plate light.

I pulled off the fancy rags casually and hung them back up, destined for the Asian Dry Cleaners Monday, really was anyone else as good at the dry cleaning? I opened all the windows and let the foggy haze of the air billow in, the misty breeze hitting my warm flesh.

I leaned out the center window and lit a cigarette, inhaling deeply, watching the vagrants in the alley, sipping from paper wrapped bottles and attempting to sneak puffs on their little glass pipes, the Devil's Dick's, the little cherries glowing bright red, illuminating their faces before fading away.

In the pre-dawn hours, only one car passed same pale tail lights, same flickering plate light. I tossed the but of the cigarette out of the window, doing my best to contribute to the filthy city I loved so much. I laid back across the futon, hitting play on the digital system, turning the volume down low and letting Bruce Springsteen sing about a woman's secret garden, I watched the ceiling fan spin as the air cooled my skin, it's breeze cooling the heat in my flesh.

I fell asleep before the second verse even began. My eyelids heavy, my mind at ease, my soul at peace.

******

I awoke with a start to loud knocking at the door; I glimpsed at a clock while pulling on a pair of grey Polo sweatpants with the blue logo. I looked at the clock and realized, even though I had just closed my eyes, most of the day had passed me by outside. I didn't bother with shoes because the knocking only seemed to continue and get louder. It could only be Jerry, my quirky neighbor from downstairs, standing at six feet tall and morbidly obese, think Comic Book Guy from the Simpsons with less hair and you would have a pretty good general idea. Jerry tended to stroll the Old City in gym shorts, a ripped Wolverine t-shirt, and a Darth Vader helmet.

"What, Jerry? Stop banging on the door," I yelled, loudly enough to be heard through the door. I flicked the lock and pulled the green door open.

Jerry wasn't even standing there. It was another man, tall, dark and handsome with a shaved head, gray eyes, and a curved chin.

Somehow I knew this rude son of a bitch with hatred in his eyes was Cynthia's husband, with the clean and pressed, yes with starch, Calvin Klein T-Shirt and stonewashed Louis Vuitton jeans, ego everywhere, coming out of his pores like the sweat that made his bald dome gleam.

Yeah, this cocky prick had to be the husband.

"I'm sorry," I said, flatly, though the process of lighting a cigarette and inhaling deeply. "I don't think I know you."

"Oh, no, my man, we haven't had the pleasure of meeting yet," he replied, his voice, deep and throaty, women would find it seductive. I found it as if he were trying to compensate for something. "But I believe you met my wife last night."

I kept the curious look, well, as much as possible when I saw him reaching behind his back, then I got a little nervous.

Okay, maybe a bit more than that, I'd had guns pulled on me in the past.

A couple of them were even fired in my direction, and it was never a real good situation, this one a little more serious, right in my doorway, and I didn't expect my door to keep him or whatever kind of slugs he had in the clip out, if I could shut it in time. A sigh of relief passed through my whole body when he pulled out an envelope, thick with cash, instead of a gun.

"Look, sir, I know you were, and I'm here to vastly overcompensate you for your services," he said, pushing the envelope into my chest, hard, but I stood my ground, didn't budge. The envelope fell to the ground; I didn't lose eye contact for an instant. "Stay away from Cynthia. I'm only going to tell you one time."

"Is that some threat," I replied, testing him.

"No, I'm too rich to threaten some whore. I have friends for that type of shit, friend. Just stay away."

"So, now I'm a whore, a friend or a sir? I'm confused and offended, well confused yes, but offended, no, not really. I'm used to the name calling from an inadequate husband or jealous boyfriend now and then."

His gaze wavered, I had won the argument with a simple comment. He turned to leave, walking briskly in the direction of Crown Plaza.

I picked up the envelope, curiously inspecting it and carried it back up the stairs to the loft, the door locking as it closed behind me.

I snubbed out the cigarette and thumbed through the bills, laughing and letting them rain down across my body like Demi Moore's sequence in Indecent Proposal.

I took the money, of course, I did, what was I, stupid? But that didn't mean I'd leave well enough alone.

The way I figured it, he had just paid me for the entire weekend, plus Monday before they left town.

The tab was paid, no bills were due. My rent and lights were taken care of for a couple of months. I'd give it a few hours for him to get some drinks in him and go on his cheating way, then give Cynthia a ring.

I laid out a Brooks Brothers Polo, crisp white with a red logo and a faded gray pair of Lacoste khaki shorts, tan ankle socks and a pair of chocolate Rockport boat shoes with brown laces, before starting the coffee machine and running hot water in the bathroom. I ran a three-disc electric shaver over my face to give myself a nice barely visible five o clock stubble. I slid off the sweatpants and boxers and climbed into the shower, the steam reminding me of the strange dream that I could grasp small details of, but no outline or fine lines were to be found. Just hints of the imagery, sensations like soft samples of the touch and feel of it all.

I scrubbed my face with a grainy, herbal cleanser, to soften the skin and camouflage the bags under my eyes from the few short hours of sleep I had received.

The Ralph Lauren body wash was scented, but faint, an excellent blend of fresh fruits with a sharp, hard liquor undertone.

I stood away from the flow of water long enough to let it all soak in, before scrubbing myself down again, erasing the remainder of Cynthia's sweet scent from my penis and short brown amber brown pubes. My balls were tight from the lack of a release last night, firm. The urge to massage myself to an orgasm and a stream of thick white ecstasy was high, but the will to hold back and spill it all deep inside of Cynthia was stronger.

When the water began to cool, I dried myself and stood in front of the mirror for a few minutes, smiling at the reflection of what I considered immaculate perfection. I splashed Giorgio Armani Acqua Di Gio on my crotch, neck and under my arms before getting dressed.

I reached for my digital watch, the only cheap watch in my collection, by the way, that gave me caller ID and text notifications but not much else, and clasped the white band around my wrist. I slid on a pair of Ralph Lauren Polo edition prescription glasses with eggshell frames, and my wardrobe was complete.

The fat little envelope of cash was filled back up and went under the kitchen sink in a key lock and combination lock safe, minus two hundred dollars in crisp new twenties that felt like they would give me paper cuts if I slid them across my flesh.

My cell phone and the cash went into the left front pocket, cigarettes, lighter and a pack of Juicy Fruit gum went to the right. I walked down the stairs and out into the hot day, making sure the door locked behind me.

Bristol's car was parked in front of the gift shop next to Old City Java, so I looked both ways and crossed, making a zig-zag around parking meters towards the store.

I felt good, I looked good, I had a feeling tonight I was going to get the chance to enjoy a woman for the pleasure alone, I needed to find her a gift.

Bristol was a punk rocker, former lead singer of Suicide Chariot, a local band that gained some fame, went on some tours and then came back home. He was five seven, maybe five eight with shoulder length black hair, sleeveless shirts, and dog collar wristbands. Most days, spikes were tossed about in his hair with careless perfection, a happy accident. He always smiled and made one feel welcome at the shop. The shop was small but carried an assortment of gifts, jewelry, and knick-knacks for young ladies and older women alike.

Bristol was behind the counter, wrapping gold dipped roses for shipping, smiling as always when I opened the door.

I waved and began perusing his shop's wares, eyes stopping on a quartz stone with the word Serenity cut into it.

The stone was smooth on top and bottom, but rough around its edges, as if the engraver had intentionally done it that way. It reminded me of the story Cynthia had told me about her love for her husband, his love for her, ad the secrets and lies within. I smiled to myself; my decision was made.

"Hey, Bristol, my man," I said, pointing to the rock in the glass case. "How's the day been treating you?"

"Well, either everybody is cheating on their wife and buying a gift to make up for it, or people are starting to remember birthdays and anniversaries," he replied, laughing while standing and grabbing the rock from the case. "They can't seem to make up their minds with the roses though. Some wanted straight up roses, which we don't carry. While others keep calling floral shops, looking for our gold and silver encrusted ones."

"Maybe if you had a website," I inquired, knowing his response.

"There is a website, Sean; you know this. Hell, you send us online business long after your "clients" are gone and away," he made the quote, unquote gesture while speaking, it was funny, in a way. Yeah, they had a website, which shipped all across America and sometimes abroad. One time, a package got sent to a cave system in the middle of some foreign desert. How the people had access to order something online from a cave system, let alone pay by card, was a mystery for the ages. RomanceHer.com was the site, but the shop was named different, Bristol and the owner fearing the casual walk-by would assume it was a dirty little sex shop, not a place to buy a necklace or stone for a recently vexed girlfriend.

"How much for the stone, my brother," I asked pulling out the handful of bills. I thumbed off one of the twenties and handed it to him while he wrapped the stone in a little brown box with a gold ribbon.

"Five bucks for you," he replied, "anybody else it's twelve." He slid the box across the table and thumbed through an envelope of cash, before handing me my change, I added it to the wad and back into the pocket the cash went. "Why are you buying a rock, man? Usually, you go extravagant."

"This one is different, Bristol," I said, smiling. "She seems like the wife that has everything, except the full attention of her husband."

"Another married lady, brother, be careful."

"Aren't I always?"

"No, Sean, you're not," he said, looking concerned. "You already forgot about the husband that sliced open your back? Or the man that put three bullets in the alley walls aiming for you?"

"No, I haven't forgotten," I said solemnly, my back itching at the thought of the scar there. The whole area had healed to a thin white line, laser surgery reducing that to a permanent white sliver whenever I take the time to get sun on my back, and the bullets, how could I forget.

Bits of concrete had scraped my face from the ricochet, embedded under my right eye for days before working themselves out of my skin.

The bullet holes were still there, in the alley, the city never really worried about things that weren't right in front of peoples faces.

I always liked to stroll the lane and see how creative the graffiti artists had gotten with them. One time, two of them had become the eyes of the dark shadow of a face, engulfed in a hood, with one fist up. It was just after the Trayvon Martin shooting, a memorial for the fallen, innocent youth. I had a photo of that one, hanging in the apartment.

"Just be careful, man," he said, going back to wrapping golden flowers. I could tell by the way he turned his back to me, the conversation was over. The deal was done, and his statement was final.

"See you later, bro."

"Yeah, whatever," he replied, his voice hollow, sorrow and agony underneath.

I could count on three fingers my real friends, and he was one of them.

I grabbed the box off the counter and exited the shop, entering Old City Java, the smells of coffee and cream filling the air. So many blends were flowing through machines, the scent reminded me of the JFG factory around the corner. I inhaled and sighed with pleasure as I ordered my house blend of the day in a paper cup and walked back outside.

Sitting at one of the little wire tables out in the alley, the only one free of rich yuppies from downtown, talking about politics and the great future ahead, unaware hours ago, their current sitting locations where the overnight homes of Knoxville's hidden people, smoking their crack pipes, drinking their liquor from a paper bag.

I pulled out my cell and checked the watch for the time before scrolling through the numbers to the C's. I hit send and let it ring twice before hanging up. Long enough for the caller ID to activate, but short enough that hopefully, only a single vibration of her phone. It was my way of contacting a client, one I had not been able to explain last night. I hoped internally that she would know the number was mine and call me back post haste. What can I say? I wanted to feel the inside of her pussy wrapped around me, stroking me, squeezing me, making me melt. I had but a taste of her last night and craved to feel her juices all over my body.

A text came through moments later, and I smiled.

******

Who is this?

It's Sean, who's this?

Cynthia, why are you texting me? Didn't Arnold come by there?

Arnold? Arnold? The guy is built like a model, and his name is Arnold? Yeah, I'd gone into stocks and bonds too, with a name like Arrrrnollllld.

Don't be mean; he said he came to see you this morning.

He did, but I didn't know if that was your feelings as well, or just his.

It's just his, but he got scary last night. I don't know what he's capable of right now. He left after he got back, took the rental, said I could call Hertz or one of those other rental places and see a movie or something, he'd be back later. But I don't know. I feel like he's watching me right now and I'm on the top floor.

Hey, calm down, it's alright. Call the rental company and when they deliver the car, come through the middle of the Old City. We can go somewhere else and talk. It will be okay, I promise.

Okay, okay, give me a couple of hours, and I'll see what I can do. You promise you'll wait for me?

I'm not going anywhere, babe.

Okay, talk to you soon.

******

I sat at the table, smiling and sipping my coffee, lighting a cigarette, wondering where I could take her. And then it dawned on me, like a light bulb going off in my head. Right around the corner, the parking lot under the interstate, it was a Saturday afternoon, the evening was already on the way, we could park in the back of the lot, be completely alone. The lot would be full before sunset, crowds moving from bar to bar, walking up the hill to the Weigels there. Nobody would think any different seeing a couple kissing in one of the cars. The lot had no lights once the sidewalk was crossed over into the entrance. That could work, I thought to myself, if he came looking, she wouldn't be at my loft, neither would I. Yeah, it was possible, it was almost too easy, the way the idea came to me.

I took another drag of the Marlboro 72 and extinguished it on the ground before tossing it into the trash bin for outside customers. The last thing I wanted to do was cause a fire across the street from my home.

I sat there and thought about the dream, attempting to remember as much of it as possible. Some of the details came easily, but the more caffeine I got into my system, the less clear the dream was. The dark imagery faded and bothered me, leaving me feeling like a forgetful man because I was at a complete loss trying to visualize something that had just happened a few short hours ago.

I went inside and paid half price on a refill, sat back down at the outdoor table and watched the people walking up and down the sidewalk, passing the time.

As the minutes turned into an hour, the crowds began to thicken.

The bars were starting to open; the air starts to cool. Instead of walking up to the loft, I walked across the street to Hannah's and ordered a Long Island Iced Tea, these people knew me, knew how I liked my drinks, knew not to try and give me the bottom shelf liquors. I watched as the cute blonde behind the counter mixed my drink and wondered why I had never taken a white woman to bed.

I kept drawing a blank when she returned with my potent concoction of liquor, and I slid her a twenty, expressing my gratitude for light ice and soda, by letting her keep the change.

I sipped the refreshing drink that made a fire in my stomach in a corner booth, watching the cars go by, the phone in my pocket went off, I glanced at my watch, and sure enough, it was Cynthia, calling this time instead of texting.

"Hello," I said, between gulps, downing the beverage and standing to leave.

"I'm in a black Lincoln Town Car, coming up the street, where are you?" Cynthia sounded nervous like I was helping to set her up or something.

"I'm down at the corner, the four-way stop," I replied, leaning on the trolley sign, looking in her direction. I saw the car and began to wave, excited with the thoughts of what was to come. She accelerated a little and pulled up beside me, hanging up her phone.

"Hey, lady, can you give me a lift?" I said, jokingly, pulling the door open and stepping inside the luxury sedan. The interior was faded gray leather, the mirror had a digital display in the bottom corner, showing an angle behind the car, a backup camera.

"Depends, sir, how far are you going?"

"Take a right," I said, easing into the seat and lighting a 72, the liquor was inside of me, loosening me up.

We passed by Hannahs and Brackins; then I had her make another right.

We pulled up to another four-way stop, and I instructed her to make another right onto Jackson Avenue, then a soft right into the parking area.

The lot was pretty full already, but there, over in the back corner, near the back side of Brackins, was an empty spot, faded light showed us the way, as the sun was beginning to set.

She used the backup camera to angle the car into the slot, rear end first. The radio was playing softly, B97.5, love songs of yesteryear hosted by Delilah. She turned off the car but left the radio on. She was dressed down today, more pure, still beautiful, still sexy. A white wife beater t-shirt from Victoria Secret, made her chocolate skin glow, a short tight blue jean skirt snug around her hips, riding her thighs, Nike Lowtop track shoes, red, with white checks and light red, almost pink ankle socks.

Cynthia turned to me, smiled softly and spoke. "I'm sorry about this morning."

"Hey, don't worry about it," I replied, offering her a 72, she accepted, and I lit the tip while she inhaled slowly. I rolled down my window and tossed mine away. "I'm used to things like that, at least he didn't come with a gun or anything."

"I know, I'm just sorry. I still don't know how he found out where you live. I don't even know where you live."

"He said he had friends around town," I commented, "maybe some of his friends know me or of me. I don't know or care. The way I see it, he doesn't even exist right now, only you and I do. Forget about him, just for a while."

Take My Breath Away by Berlin came on the radio, Cynthia turned it up, puffed slowly on her cigarette and lip sang the song.

I could see the tears at the edges of her eyes, wanted to reach over, wipe them away, kiss her, hold her, push myself inside of her and get lost in her. But I didn't want to interrupt her moment, lose the connection, kill the vibe inside of her. She sighed softly and tossed the butt out of her window as the song ended.

"Sean."

"Yes, Cynthia," I replied, reaching over and turning her face towards mine, our eyes making contact for the first time since I had gotten in the car.

"Can we get out of this car? I feel like it's smothering me," she asked.

"Smothering you? This car is as big as my loft," I said with a half smile, expecting her to laugh.

When she didn't, I opened my door and walked around the car, opening hers so she could stand. We sat on the trunk of the car, still warm from the fading sun, and watched people on the patio behind Brackin's, drinking and laughing, dancing to songs that whispered in the air around us.

"Why isn't my life as simple as theirs, Sean? Why isn't yours?"

"How do we know their lives are simple, Cynthia? For all you know, their lives are as complicated as ours, as difficult to traverse as a stunt and test track. For example, that young girl over there, dancing the hardest, yelling the loudest, I bet she is the most troubled of them all. Shitty life is just a part of the living thing now. We'll never have it as easy or as clean as the people in the 70s and 80s did. Too much has changed, the population has grown too much."

"I'm just tired of feeling like I'm missing out on something fresh, something better," she said, taking my hand in hers. "I want to go out, experience life like he has, go to foreign countries, eat exotic foods where they originated from, not from an expensive deli in Times Square."

"Then why don't you," I asked, she placed my hand on her thigh and moaned as I squeezed and massaged the flesh there. She lifted her booty off the trunk enough for the skirt to rise to her hips, exposing naked flesh, a light coating of fuzz on the inside. She eased my hand up further and held it close, her hips squeezing my hand as I massaged her leg, my thumb extended, glancing touches across the fuzz, the opening, her little button, protruding from between her lips.

"I'm going to," she sighed, releasing her hips and giving my hand access to her opening, heat washing over it as my fingers spread her labia, my middle sliding deep inside. "When we return to New York, I'm pulling my money out of our accounts and starting a separate one and hiring a lawyer."

"You should," I said before kissing the flesh of her neck, my finger probing her opening, sliding in and out of her, rubbing circles around her anus, making her filthy orchid moist with the juices running down the crack of her ass. She moaned when I teased it, applying pressure, the tip of my finger squeezed tightly by her booty. I wanted to press deeper, see how she responded, opening her up, two fingers, two openings. But I held back, kissed her lips, massaged her pussy lips, teasing her, making her moan.

"I'm going to," she cried through gritted teeth, gripping at my shorts, squeezing me, rubbing me through the fabric. "I don't think I would have been able to if you hadn't come into my life. You make me feel brave, Sean. You force me to feel alive. You remind me of what being touched should feel like, instead of repeated motions all the time."

I lifted one of her plump breasts out of the wife beater, her chocolate skin showing the white material, caressing it, kissing the nipple, sucking it gently. My other hand feeling around her firm little vagina, caressing the outer lips, glancing touches across her clitoris, and little inner labia lips. I teased her with my hand, gently rubbing circles around her clitoris, sliding down, deep, soaking my finger and coming back up to twirl the circles again.

"I want you to kiss it," she cooed. Her hands were running across the stubble on top of my head, her voice hoarse with pleasure. "Can you kiss my pussy, Sean?"

I kissed her lips gently, easing off the trunk of the car, she laid back, her upper body pressed against the glass, her head arched, resting on the roof, staring at the stars between the spaces of the interstate above. She put her feet on the bumper and lifted her hips enough to pull the skirt up over her hips and around her waist.

Her dripping vagina, spread open, pink, squeezing and releasing, anticipating the feeling of my breath, my tongue massaging it. I stood back and admired her beauty, lighting a cigarette. She looked up at me, eyes looking like a fiend in need of a fix, pleasure in her face.

Cynthia rubbed her nipples, pulling the other breast free of her wifebeater. One hand ventured down her belly, between her thighs, I watched, taking it all in, as she rubbed her crotch for me, her fingers playing her clit and pussy lips like a fleshy instrument. The way her fingers slid in and out, up and down, the way she squirmed, the gasps, the moans, I watched as I smoked my cigarette, enjoying the vision before me. I massaged my shorts with my left hand, the hardness visible to her yearning eyes. She began to slow her fingers, tighten her thighs. I shook my head, tossing the cigarette away.

I took a step forward and pulled her thighs apart, watching the fingers, jealous of their magic, I put her legs over my shoulders and pulled her pussy close to my face. I went to work like the professional I was, licking her clitoris, sucking on her labia, gently nibbling at her fat little outer lips. I forced my tongue between the clenching walls of her opening, the flavors reminding me of cactus fruit and mango, the walls relaxed, a line of warm juice freeing and clinging to my facial hair. She was cumming for me; her fingers dug into my scalp, her hips bucked, rocking the Lincoln, the thighs squeezed me close. I sang a song of love to her pussy in the form of saliva and strokes of the tongue, vibrations relaxing, the clenches increasing again.

Again she came, and again I drank, like a vampire at her veins.

Her toes caressed my crotch, I took it as an invitation, unzipped the shorts and slid them and the boxers down, around my knees.

Her toes touched me, as much as was possible, attempting to wrap themselves around me. I softly pushed her foot away and stood, pulling her close to me, her ass hanging in the air for an instant, before I entered her, all the way, deep. I eased her back onto the trunk and began giving her the slow strokes and deep pushes.

"I, I can't," she moaned out, her pussy telling me otherwise.

"Yeah, you can," I assured her, kissing her lips and lifting her off the trunk of the car and turning around, still deep inside her.

I eased back against the car and let her ride me while I gripped her around the waist, her strokes, reverse to the head then slamming into me.

Claps of lust in the night, she went fast, she went slow, she grinded against me when she came again and begged me to let her down.

She bent over the trunk, hands pulling her ass cheeks wide, her pink throbbing opening pleading with me to push deep inside again.

Like a true quarterback, I took a knee and buried my face between, my tongue running circles around her little rosebud of an anus and back to her pussy, teasing them both, pushing deep in her vagina and nibbling at her ass cheeks. She moaned with pleasure as I stood again, entering her slowly, juice and pressure attempting to push me back out. I gripped at her neck and stood her up as she ground her pussy against me from the back. One of her hands found its way between her legs, switching between stroking my balls and rubbing her clit. She came again, hard. I nibbled on her neck and turned her head, kissing her deeply.

"It's okay, Sean," she cooed.

"He made me get fixed years ago." She let out a sob that faded to moans after a few grinds against me.

I pulsed inside of her.

I wanted it too, to spill, to release, to melt and mold into each other like lava in a lamp.

I eased out of her wet opening, she gasped, spun, looking at me.

I lifted her back onto the hood and pressed inside her wetness, moaning. She put her head on my shoulder, and we rocked slowly, I could feel the build-up deep inside and grabbed her ass again, lifting her up. I kissed her then, deep in the mouth, teeth, and tongue, my hands lifting and dropping her hips slowly and deeply, I spun and pushed her against the chainlink fence. She gripped the rail above her head and pushed down on my cock, hard but slow, profound and wet, she looked to the sky and gasped, her orgasm rocking again. I felt the urge and let go. My seed was spilling deep inside her, shot after shot of smooth white tequila into the throat of life. I saw fireworks in her eyes and splashes of light in the sky as I came with her, she released the fence and held me tight, her pussy massaging every last drop out of me, her juices running down our thighs.

.

Cynthia began to cry on my shoulder as I eased out of her and carried her back to the car, setting her down and lifting her face to mine. I kissed her lips softly once before the first shot rang out, glass shattering, people still partying at the clubs behind the lot. At first, I thought it was a loud radio, or in some place, off in the distance, across the city or the planet. The second shot told me it was much closer, too close. The back window of the Lincoln busted out, spraying Cynthia's back and my face with glass. The shots were targeted at someone near us, or so I thought. The third loud bang and flash of light, impact sounded closer. Still, sparks flew off the trunk of the car. Cynthia gasped as I pulled her close to me and down onto the hard pavement of the parking lot. Through the shattered glass of the car windows, I could hear the guitar solo of Guns N Roses "Don't Cry" playing on the radio. A car door opened, under the car I could see feet, racing in our direction. Slowing when they reached the car, coming from the side in slow motion. Shots four and five came from above us, a ski mask, gold teeth, pressure in my stomach. The seventh and final shot bouncing off the concrete beside me, Cynthia rolled off of me and gasped. Footsteps were retreating, Cynthia with labored breathing. Another set of approaching footsteps, somebody else to finish the job.

I turned my head to face Cynthia, my body aching, not moving.

I reached out and took her hand, gasping at what I saw, screaming.

Her face lying sideways on the pavement, one eye bulging at me but still moving, her throat making sounds, choking on her blood.

She mouthed words, nothing came out of her lips, but a giant bubble of dark red blood, that popped splattering my face. I turned to see the man approaching, struggling to move, to make some stand, my body not willing to respond. There stood her husband, looking both heartbroken and smug, a length of pipe in his gloved hand.

"I told you to leave her alone, you son of a bitch," he screamed, bringing the pipe down once across my chest, twice, the side of my face, breaking the skin, shattering bone, salty blood filling my mouth. A third time, the side of my head. I coughed harshly, blood spilling from my mouth, he turned, ran away. And like a movie, a movie based on real life and not some shitty romantic comedy. Everything got bright and loud and faded to black.

Nightmares & Realities

"That amazing grace, though it passed you by."

"You wake up every day, and you start to cry."

"You wanna die, but you just can't quit."

Let me break it down, it's the fucked up shit."

My Shit's Fucked, Up-Warren Zevon

Time passed slower than I thought humanly possible, consciousness came and went, the darkness seemed to be my new home, there was no way to tell how long I lay there, body growing cold in the summer heat, the party still going on across the way.

Cynthia laid out near me, eyes no longer moving, face looking worse than when I first passed out.

I faded out again, like some cheap movie with bad editing, the images in my mind, her beautiful face shattered and broken, flesh hanging away in some places, bone and pink meat pushing through in others. The hard concrete became air, then a mattress of sorts, the pain was as constant to my body like breathing, images on repeat in my mind, sleepless darkness filled with vivid imagery. Cynthia was laying there, one eye pressed forward, blood leaking from her mouth and nose, glass peppering the ground around her.

Lights, bright, shinning, pressure on my face, labored breathing made easier, pain receding, sleep becoming more of an option, faces veered in masks, voices talking, fade to darkness, images of my mother, alive and well, smoking a cigarette.

Marlboro Ultra-Light 100, sitting on her fluffy black leather couch. Laughing and smiling, the light behind her, Bristol bent over me, shaking his head, Essence crying, leaning in, kissing my forehead, fade to darkness.

I awake in a pool of warm water, hints of chlorine and salt in the air, naked, a full moon above me, surrounded by fluffy white clouds looking pregnant with water, ready to spill down in moments notice.

Naked women of all shapes and sizes, swam around me, laying by the sides of the pool. Skin tones from dark chocolate to faded caramel, nipples the size of pennies and nipples the areolas the size of silver dollars, all beautiful in their ways.

Asses vast and round, the size of a juicy rump roast, some as small as a pair of pineapples, equally beautiful, passed by me in the water, some brushed against my flesh, most just passing me by in a sensual coordinated rhythm.

Slow circles they swam around me, some taking me in their mouths, some kissing my legs and back, my body an underwater easel for their fine arts and a blank page for their lips and tongues to paint. One of them rose above the water's edge before me, water dripping from her hair and flesh, her eyes as green as gems in the sunlight, looking like a great goddess. She came to me, her dark chocolate skin looking as melted as the drops of water that dripped from the curve of her chin, the tips of her erect nipples. She took me into her arms, pulled me close, made me feel alive.

Her jade eyes glowed through the darkness, the rest of her face, hidden in the shadows. Clouds in the sky began to rumble as she welcomed me into her body, thunder rolled as her hips began to buck against me. Raindrops, cold and round, pelted my flesh as she arched her back, her hands squeezing her large breasts, moans escaped my lips as she rose, lightning flaring in the sky, illuminating her misshapen face, blood leaking out of her mouth, her nose, her ears. Cynthia stared back at me through the darkness.

The water began to be cold, the warmth was gone from the air, the rain started to change into ice pellets and snowflakes, everything around us becoming a blinding white, the other women vanished from sight, one by one, each with a pop, like a balloon.

The water froze around our waists, my arms locked under the ice, still grasping her gracious hips and delicious ass, the only warmth under the water, where our crotches were joined together. Cynthia's breasts sat above the ice, as did her arms. She tried to say something, something important through the blood, and I could sense the urgency in the way her body gripped mine, only bubbles came forth, popping and splattering my face with warm red droplets. She sobbed and bowed her head.

Cynthia ran her fingers over her bloody tongue and wrote two words in a macrabe font of chicken scratch, seeming to glow out of the pristine white ice that had surrounded us. I didn't want to read them; I wanted to hold her close as long as I could, so that maybe we could live, at this moment forever. She took my head in her cool hands, chilling me to the bone, turning it slowly towards the ice. And suddenly, everything seemed to make sense.

WAKE UP was written there in her precious blood, I shook my head and sobbed, the tears freezing on my face almost instantly, my eyes rose and met hers. Cynthia leaned forward and kissed my lips, her blood seeping through my mouth, warmth in the cold, and then, as if touched by an angel, I woke up.

To say I awoke, fully aware, would be a gross exaggeration. I was dazed and confused, stuck in a cloudy slumber, awake but not really. The room as cold and bare, white, sanitized, a hospital. My lids lifted hazily, the energy I didn't feel I had, required to raise them. Machines beeped slowly and steadily around me, attached to my skin, IVs were plugged into different veins in my arms, I became more aware, the hospital room was no longer a guess, but a clear realization. I felt drunk as if I hadn't been out very long, maybe just hours, realizing it was probably whatever pain medication they had me on, making me feel this way. Weakness was not something I was used to or comfortable with, stuck in place, trapped with no control over my bodily functions or limbs. The lights were bright, seemingly blinding in their glare, adding a shadow in the darkness behind my lids when they'd close. The air around me, cold, wet on the throat and lungs.

Fading out of consciousness again, a softer feeling, more surreal, more of a state of being, a world within my own. Colors were brighter; my flesh felt itchy, aches came and went in an instant. I felt a cool wash over me, a burn in my arm. Again I slept, realizing this was a waking moment, not some horrible nightmare, everything in the parking lot had happened, not very long ago, and reality was this hospital room around me. I fought the hazy feeling, to the best of my ability, I lost the battle in a few moments. The clouds were setting in on the beach of my mind, voices coming closer. Unaware if they were in my opinion, on the beach with me, or in the hospital room, observing me.

"Do you think he'll wake up?"

"I don't know," replied a familiar voice. "It's stated the draining is helping, working the blood out of his lungs, but nothing is certain at this point."

I began to fade away again. But this time, no dreams came, just bitter darkness, never-ending and all-consuming.

******

When I awoke again, my mother was sitting across the room in the noisy green pullout chair, smiling and talking to a male nurse, scratch that, he was a doctor, judging by his attire and relaxed demeanor. I had spoken with him before, and his name was Ed, he had longish manicured fingernails and red hair, pulled back in a tight ponytail, those are the things I remembered the most about Ed. His face was smooth, unblemished; women would find Ed attractive for a redhead, probably even beautiful. Ed glanced my way, winked at me, grinned and laughed with my mother, patting her on the leg and then kissing her on the cheek before standing and walking into the hall.

"You know, Sean, I like him," my mother said, digging in her beat-up brown leather purse, probably looking for a Merit Ultra-Light 100 or a Goody powder. "He had some nice things to say about you, some of them, actually made a lot of sense."

My mother was a short, skinny woman in her late 50s, white hair that was more yellow than gray and a list of medical and mental issues from years of drug abuse followed by life catching up with her early. She had spent too many years alone in her trailer, too many nights alone on her beat-up black leather and gray stitched couch. My mom lit up one of her cigarettes right there in the room and looked out the window, looking beautiful for just a moment, at the city of Perryville.

"Mom, why are you here," I asked, nervously, wondering when the doctors or a nurse would kick in the door, demanding she extinguishes the cancer stick.

"I'm here because it's not your time yet, son," she replied hitting her cigarette, smoke exiting her nose and mouth while her look was sullen and severe.

"I don't understand," I replied, lost in a haze, the IV in my arm again taking control of me.

"Ed needs to talk to you, Sean. About Cynthia and yourself, about life, about death," she responded cryptically, in a strange code. "He has an offer for you. It may not seem like a possibility, but Ed can deliver, Sean."

"Mom, Ed can't be real," I said, emotional at the words coming out of my mouth, "if he was talking to you, he could not be real."

My mother looked hurt as she had after so many of our conversations in the past. One of us angry at the experiences, the other trying to apologize. Her eyes screamed to the Heavens for tears, and her lips trembled. Another apology was on her mouth, one I would hear, but I would not accept. Because sometimes, some things just cannot be let go.

"And why can't Ed be real, Sean," she asked, barely keeping the composure she was fighting to grasp.

"Because," I sobbed, "because you're dead."

I mumbled it out more than speaking it aloud before everything began to fade again, tears in my eyes and sorrow in my heart.

"But you're not, son, you're alive. Go back to the real world. Talk with Doctor Ed; he can help you, son."

My mother kissed my cheek and began to fade away as I faded away into sleep. The darkness consumed me again, space, timeless, infinite, silent and hollow.

******

When I opened my eyes again, Ed was standing in the corner, talking to Essence and Bristol, chatting them up while a nurse checked my vitals and wrote down the information. I tried to speak but my throat was dry, a tube inserted into it.

I choked and tried to pull it out, the padded cuffs on my wrists holding me down. The nurse realized I was awake, aware, conscious and gagging on the feeding tube in my throat. Ed began approaching me, and I flinched, nervous that I was still asleep.

"Now, now, Sean," he said, his voice oddly soothing. "Calm down."

"I'm just going to remove the tube now. You may feel a slight pull, just close your eyes and try not to vomit, ok?"

I nodded and closed my eyes, at first I felt a tickle in my throat, the pressure, it felt like my organs were attached to the small skinny tube, I choked and gasped, waited for the feeling of suffocation and to taste my blood, but the feelings never came.

I opened my eyes again to find Ed standing there with Bristol and Essence close by, both of my friends, crying with joy or sorrow, I couldn't tell which.

"Would one of you please go get a cup of ice from the nurse's station, I'm pretty sure our friend here needs it?"

Essence nodded and opened the door, a tidbit of the BeeGee's "I Surrender" whispering through the doorway from the nurse's station. Bristol came over and shook my hand, smiling.

"You never take my advice," Bristol said, smiling but with a slight frown on it.

"Do I ever," I responded, dryly, before coughing for nearly a minute. Essence returned with the ice, handing it to me, humming the tune of that BeeGees song. I greedily took chunks of the ice into my mouth, chewing them to dust, letting them melt and moisten my tongue and cool my dry throat.

"We'll be back in the morning, boo," Essence said, kissing my cheek. "The doctor has questions, and so do the police."

"Thank you," I whispered, trying not to go into another coughing fit. They both made little waves of the hand and exited the room, leaving me alone with Ed, the ever-grinning doctor, who shut the door and sat on the edge of my bed.

"You've been in and out of an induced coma for over a week," he said as if it were all normal. Being a doctor, it probably was normal to him. "We had to place a drip line in your lung to drain the blood.

"Blood?"

"Do you not remember anything, Sean?"

"Bits and pieces, flashes of things, but I can't tell what's real and what's just in my head."

"Let me tell you what all we treated," Ed replied, smiling devilishly, "See if that jogs your memory."

I nodded, slightly hesitant, chewing more of the ice.

"Blunt force trauma to the skull, causing a slight concussion, we drilled a small hole to release the pressure and swelling.

You're lucky it didn't kill you. A dislocated jaw, the easiest thing to fix on the list. Two cracked ribs, a third rib broken, pierced your lung, hence the drip lines."

"The parking lot in the Old City, behind Barley's," I said, suddenly remembering all of the details, the passion, the pain, Cynthia laying beside me on the ground. Dr. Ed nodded as I tried to get the question out. "Cynthia, is she?"

Ed's face turned deathly serious as he nodded one last time, adding a certain creepy finality to it all.

"Multiple gunshot wounds to the body and head, numerous lacerations to the head, presumably from the same object that were used in the assault against you."

"Her husband did it," I replied, no other words would come, I turned my head and sobbed, her shattered face, stuck in my mind, smiling and bloody.

"Mr. Hart claims innocence, has a list of places he visited in New York the night in question.

Witness list an inch thick, he returned to New York with her body, three days ago," Ed said, shaking his head at no one in particular. "The detectives are on their way, questions and answers are to be given. Talk to them, but leave him out of it. After they leave, we will talk again."

******

Ed was right, the police came in, asked a lot of questions, gave only a few answers, stated that two suspects were in custody and the case, by their standards, was closed. I did as ED said and left the parts about her husband out of it, ignoring the desire to correct them, argue for some semblance of justice for Cynthia. But the words would not come. The two detectives left, the drip dropped, again and again, I was in the mellow darkness again, the chords of Guns N Roses echoing in my mind.

******

Dreams, dreams are things that we make in our minds, our subconscious is trying to tell us something, at least that's what I've been told a time or two. Well if that's the case, I wish these dreams of mine would stop beating around the bush and come out and tell me what they have to say. Exhaustion from being awake so long had mixed with alcohol and left me there on the futon, in the sense of being I imagined to be like a good LSD trip.

All of the colors around me were brighter than normal as if they had sucked in the sun's rays and glowed with majestic light.

The grass seemed to be almost neon around me, the sand at the edge of the water was golden and shiny like a mirage.

The waves were crashing into the sand, each one shaped like a woman from my past, a hidden message behind the wet symbolism. The water a blue so clear that the foam was almost crystal clear. And the sky, not even blue, hues of green, orange, purple and yellow.

A short gentleman in a red vest and black slacks offered me a silver tray with multiple cigars and a small bottle of tequila. I smelled through them all, picking the one that smelled the most robust. The little bottle of Patron I carried with me, the cork left behind in the sand. I felt as if I had been walking for an eternity, searching for someone, something. The man produced a cigar cutter from thin air, as if by magic, and sliced away the end of the cigar.

I put it to my lips, and he produced an expensive looking wooden match, striking it against his thumbnail. The cigar had the scent and taste of a true bonafide Cuban before it was lit, but when I took in the first pull of that delicious aromatic smoke, my senses said something entirely different. The taste I recognized was a Black and Mild with a wooden tip. The man laughed as if reading my thoughts and pointed to my hand, which held one of the cigarillos, not the cigar I had chosen from his fancy tray. I took the this as a sign and continued to puff on the cigarillo and sipping from the little square shaped bottle while walking along the beach.

I watched the waves, images of past lovers, caught in their crashing shapes, the foam welling up and reaching for me. I looked back to see if my friend, the server, was seeing this too, but he was gone, not even a footprint in the sand. I was alone on the beach. I felt exhausted as if this journey was nearing its end, so I sat in the sand and watched the waves crash and the not exactly a solar orb in the sky sink on the horizon. The colors were seeming to blend, waiting to set the ocean ablaze.

The sand welcomed me, beckoned me to lay down, so I did, watching the sky change colors before me like some secret solar storm nobody was supposed to see.

The sand wasn't grainy, but soft, inviting.

I relaxed and let the dream take hold, the ground around me coming to life, massaging my tired flesh.

I smoked the cigarillo and imagined it was her fingers caressing me, touching the tender spots in my muscles and rubbing them lose. I was like putty in her fingers, my flesh meshing and molding between her hands. The tide had risen, soft sprays cooling my hot flesh. I looked up to see a woman of water, walking my way, naked and transparent.

Her hair was made of the breaks bubbly foam, sitting atop her head like fluffy bulbs of cotton, as white as the clouds. She came to me, sat by my side and sipped from my bottle of tequila; I saw the fluid running down inside her and mixing with the water that was her shape. She passed me the bottle, and I sipped, long and hard, swallowing it all, tasting salt on the rim.

I closed my eyes again and felt her watery touch on my flesh, caressing me, welcoming me into total euphoria as she touched and rubbed my chest and neck.

Made in the USA
Columbia, SC
27 December 2024

48566475R00083